The Mensch

Leopold Borstinski

Published by Sobriety Press
Cover design and Illustrations by James, GoOnWrite.com
Edited by Melanie Underwood
##

ISBN 978 1 913313 45 6 ePub Edition
ISBN 978 1 913313 44 9 Kindle Edition
ISBN 978 1 913313 46 3 Paperback Edition

For more information please visit LeoB.ws

##

June 1975

1

ALEX COHEN STEPPED out of the shower and stared out of the bedroom window. All was quiet. The only discernible sounds were of his wife, Sarah, rattling in the kitchen preparing breakfast. It had been a long few weeks, and he was glad to be home safe, knowing that she was there for him, after all these years.

When he contemplated his life, he lingered on the friends he had lost, like Arnold Rothstein, Charlie Lucky, and Alfonse Capone. The fellas from the days of Prohibition and the opportunities that sprang up around America after the government bent to the people's will and allowed liquor back in the country. His mind seldom considered the hundreds he had killed: Abe Reles, the Murder Corporation rat, or Benny Siegel, who had saved him when he'd left Sing Sing but had stolen money from the Italian mob. In fact, the only person whose death still haunted him was the sixteen-year-old who took a bullet between the eyes in the trenches of France during the Great War. And the army had given him a Purple Heart for that.

Alex got dressed and slipped downstairs into the kitchen. Sarah smiled at him, poured a mug of coffee, and passed it to him.

"I thought it would be nice for us to eat on the patio this morning."

"Like old times, Sarah."

He beamed and gave her a peck on the cheek while making sure not to spill his drink.

◆ ◆ ◆

ALEX GLANCED UP from his paper and pointed at the picture on the front page. "Have you seen this?"

The photo showed a stream of Vietnamese clambering up a ladder hoping to escape from Saigon in a US military helicopter.

Sarah's eyes glanced at the image, but she couldn't make herself stare for too long.

"I can't imagine what it's like fighting in the jungles of Vietnam, Sarah."

"Does this bring it all back?"

Alex nodded and reached out to hold her hand. The Great War was civilized compared to what he had seen on television in the last few years. Everything had gone downhill since Kennedy was assassinated.

"Let's not dwell in the past, Alex. Just remind yourself that we live together, we love together, but we die alone."

"I know. I guess I'm sad that it has come to this." He flicked the newspaper. "America was supposed to be the land of milk and honey when we arrived at Ellis Island. Instead, it has shipped tens of thousands of boys off to be slaughtered and sent pictures home every night to show us what is being done in our name."

"Alex, you almost sound patriotic. I thought your concerns were limited to our family and your business interests."

"Most of the time, but now and again…"

Sarah allowed her husband to wallow in his thoughts for a few minutes, and then she poured him another mugful. She lit a cigarette and passed it to him. Alex took three long drags and returned to the present. When he finished the smoke, he smiled and tucked into his breakfast: cereal, a bagel with smoked salmon, and two cheese blintzes washed down with a large glass of orange juice and coffee.

◆ ◆ ◆

"WHERE'S VERONICA?"

Sarah laughed.

“We gave the housekeeper the day off. That way, we could spend some time alone together.”

A nod and Alex stared down into his lap.

“I’ve been a disappointment to you for so long, Sarah.”

“Do not talk like that, Alex Cohen. Yes, you made some mistakes along the line, but you also did your best to be a good father to our children and be a provider to this family.”

“Will you ever forgive me, Sarah?”

“I told you I’ve done so already. If I had not, you wouldn’t be sitting at this table. You’d still be back in Palm Springs. Let’s not rehash old arguments. What’s done is done and we have the rest of our lives ahead of us. Together.”

“Thank you, Sarah.”

“Alex, if you can’t move beyond this, we will never be happy again. You must acknowledge what you have done to yourself and accept the past for what it is. I know I am doing my best to, and you must do so too.”

He nodded and stood up, gave her a kiss on the lips, and mumbled about getting more of his affairs in order. Sarah remained on the patio and smoked another cigarette before taking the breakfast things into the kitchen and washing them up. Alex appeared from his office on the far side of the summerhouse, which was opposite the pool.

“I don’t know what time I’ll be home.”

“That’s fine. You’ll be back as soon as you can.”

“You got any plans, Sarah?”

“I might take a swim this morning and visit the boys this afternoon.”

“Twenty years ago, you told me off for still thinking of them as boys.”

“Correct, but it’s a mother’s right to always think of her children as her babies.”

Alex smiled, kissed her goodbye, and walked out the front door. Sarah shuffled back onto the patio and slumped onto a sunbed. She shut her eyes for a second.

As soon as her eyelids were closed, the walls of the house shook and the windows rattled. A bang and the smell of burning metal and rubber. She ran to the front; Alex's car was a fireball. Sarah slumped onto the grass and screamed.

December 1970

2

ALEX SAT DOWN to breakfast and consumed the blintzes, orange juice, and the rest of his meal. Sarah remained opposite him at the kitchen table with a single slice of toast and a small amount of butter in stark contrast to her husband. As soon as he finished a plate, she whipped it away from him and returned to her chair.

Then she rose again and grabbed the pot of coffee and topped up Alex's mug, and sat down. Then up to seize the side *shissel* that housed his bagel. He peered over his newspaper.

"Is there something the matter, hon? You seem jittery this morning."

Sarah picked up plates and plopped them nearer the sink. Then she topped up the mugs again after she sat down.

"I'm just worried, Alex."

"What about?"

"This is difficult for me to say because I don't want you to get annoyed."

"Now why would I do that? When was the last time I was even angry in your presence, let alone at you? Spill."

She took a large sip of her coffee before opening her mouth.

"You've talked about retiring for quite a while and I wondered if you'd got any closer to deciding when that will be."

"Sarah, it's a work in progress, you know that."

She smirked for a second.

"You've been threatening to divest your illegal interests since we fled Cuba, and here we are. Our sons are waiting to take over the legitimate family business and your lieutenants want to see you step away too."

"Really? I can't recall the last time we even spoke about my retirement."

"Alex, that's because Ezra and Massimo don't wish to show you any disrespect. But you must appreciate they want to run Vegas without you."

He felt the hairs on the back of his neck stand on edge as he heard Sarah's words.

"Besides, Alex, we are not getting any younger. You might not have been involved in any hits for a while, but that doesn't mean I'm not concerned whether you'll return in one piece each time you visit Vegas or Atlantic City."

Alex whistled.

"I haven't had a contract to fulfill since '68. Those days are behind me. How long have you been bottling all this up, Sarah?"

"It's not that my every waking minute has been filled with these thoughts, but we are all waiting for the day when you step aside. For your own safety, if nothing else."

Alex chewed on the last mouthful of bagel and pushed the remains of his blintzes around his plate with a fork.

"Meyer phoned me yesterday."

"Oh? What did he have to say for himself?"

"He called from Israel."

"Did you know he was going on vacation?"

"It's not that, Sarah. Uncle Sam is indicting him for tax evasion, so he has left the country before they slam him in jail."

"Lansky has been so careful over the years with all his financial affairs. I should know because I took care of his accounts for a decade."

"The charges pre-date your involvement. They go back to the time of Benny Siegel and the Flamingo Hotel."

It was Sarah's turn to let out a slow whistle.

"Isn't that ancient history by now?"

"For you and me it is, but not for the federal authorities. The trouble is that if they find Meyer guilty, then he'll end his days behind bars. He has almost nothing; his family members own his assets."

"Is Thelma out there with him?"

"Yes, his wife couldn't stay here without him. They have no idea how long it will be before he can come back to Florida."

"And, Alex, you consider this is a reason to maintain a grip on your criminal empire? To me, that is the strongest argument there is for you to get out of the business before it bites you on the ass."

He shrugged because he knew Sarah was right, but there was something about those monthly payments from Ezra and Massimo that he didn't want to let go of.

3

ALEX ANNOUNCED AN extraordinary general meeting of the family business. Present were Sarah, their sons David and Moishe, and Alex's sister, Esther. Their offices were a standalone building on the grounds of the Hibiscus Island mansion that Alex and Sarah called home now they had moved to Miami.

"When I announced to you all that we were going to relocate from Hollywood to the East Coast, I made several promises: that we would leave behind some of my business interests, that I would spend more time with my family, and that Sarah and I would marry."

"One for three isn't bad, Pop."

Alex scowled at his accountant Moishe. He might be younger than his lawyer brother, but he was still fresh at almost every opportunity. And he grew worse as he became older.

"The good news is that I've made inroads to extricate myself from some of my illegitimate enterprises, but it continues as a work in progress."

Everybody nodded in agreement and shuffled papers in front of them. The brothers had been waiting a lifetime to take over their father's business, although they had only been up to the task in the last few years, at least in Alex's eyes.

AT LUNCHTIME, SARAH and Alex ate together while the others stayed over at the pool by the main house.

"Alex, what are we going to do about Ezra and Massimo?"

"Huh?"

"How long will they be prepared to wait for you to hand over control of Vegas to them?"

"They're earning well. What's the hurry?"

"Alex, if you keep people hanging on for long enough, then they'll take matters into their own hands."

"Don't be ridiculous, Sarah. Those two men are more loyal to me than any other fella has been in my life. Even the likes of Meyer."

"Loyalty only goes so far, Alex. At the end of the day, guys want to put food on the table and keep a roof over their heads. Promises don't pay the bills."

He fell silent and pondered. He had been talking about going straight for more years than he cared to remember. Perhaps Sarah was right, again.

"How much time before things turn ugly?"

"You know there's no straightforward answer to that."

"Apart from Vegas, there is the wire service, and my gaming and hotel interests in Atlantic City and Los Angeles."

"Alex, is that really all that's left?"

"The monthly payments from those three ventures keep us in clover. I haven't had to touch the money we got out of Cuba because of that cash flow."

"Including the wire service?"

"Well, you might think that it has had its day, but it still earns, even now. Most of the income is from smaller bookies as the large organizations use televised sports to give them firsthand information without our help."

"So, offering that to Ezra and Massimo would be more of an insult than anything else."

"That's the size of it."

"And AC?"

"Now that is a different matter, Sarah. There are at least a dozen hotels and more casinos than that under my influence. On top of that, there are the bookies who pay tribute too."

"And did we leave anything in LA that is worth mentioning?"

"I gave our Los Angeles prostitution operation to Massimo and narcotics went to Ezra when we got married. But I ran a protection racket around Tinseltown after I resolved the union business for United Studios, and that is more than chump change."

IN THE AFTERNOON, the family reconvened in the boardroom.

"I'd forgotten this room existed."

"What are you talking about, Moishe?"

"I'm not being funny, but I reckon this is the first time since we moved to Florida that we have held a meeting of the directors. And I don't believe I've ever noticed this place even being here. What about the rest of you?"

Shrugs all round as the others acknowledged Moishe's observation.

"The second floor is under-utilized, Moishe, but you are all welcome to come up here at any time."

"Now that we are here, what is there to discuss, Alex?"

David brought the conversation to a more practical place than his brother's aside.

"I want everyone to prepare for a more active role."

"Pop, is this a repeat of this morning's bold claims by you? No disrespect, but I'll believe it when I see it."

Alex scowled at Moishe, and Sarah raised her eyes to heaven.

"Are these just empty words, my son?"

"Not at all, Pop. But I don't understand how we can prepare for something when we have no idea what it's going to look like or what you expect of us."

"You and David need to consider our corporate structure: how many subsidiaries are best for us to minimize our tax position, and what areas might you wish to expand into? Matters along those lines."

"Doesn't all this depend on what you want us to do, Alex?"

"Not at all, Esther. Part of the new order is for me to step down from any day-to-day activities. My intention is to take income from the business but not involve myself with any of the decision making. This will be run by you and your nephews."

Esther's eyes shifted left and right. Sarah smiled at her.

"Your strengths are figuring out the optimum systems and procedures the company should operate under. So once David and Moishe resolve the high finance, you can figure out the best way we all function on a daily basis."

Alex heard an audible sigh of relief from his sister.

"Besides, Esther, we aren't vanishing in a puff of smoke. Both Sarah and I will be available for as long as you need us to be. We're only a short walk away from this building."

He pointed out of the window toward the mansion, whose roof was visible above the tree line. Esther nodded and took a glug of her coffee.

4

ALEX FLEW OVER to Palm Springs, where he kept a house to hold meetings with his lieutenants without being in sight of any Italians in Las Vegas. Gangster Sam Giancana had warned him the mob would not tolerate his presence anywhere near their operations after the unauthorized death of Bobby Kennedy.

"Thanks for meeting with me at such short notice. I know you two fellas are busy managing our interests in Nevada."

Ezra smiled for a moment and Massimo lit a cigarette. They remained silent, making Alex put all the effort into the conversation.

"I have been slower than any of us imagined possible to divest myself from our mutual business concerns and I must admit it is still a work in progress..."

Massimo took a loud drag of his smoke while Ezra remained with a fixed half-grin on his face.

"But I assure you my intention remains to hand over control of Vegas to you two fellas. There is nobody I trust more to grow this enterprise."

The Italian stubbed the remnants of his cigarette. Ezra sipped from his drink and was the first to respond.

"No disrespect, Alex, but did you invite us over to Palm Springs to say you'll keep to your word someday?"

Alex swallowed. He had not expected Ezra to be so direct with him nor to be so negative. Sarah was right, their patience had worn thin.

"I also reckoned we'd talk how the Feds have indicted Meyer on tax evasion charges. They date back to the days of Benny Siegel."

Ezra whistled in surprise.

"Those guys just won't let go of the past, will they?"

"No, it's a long time since Bobby Kennedy was attorney general, but that doesn't mean the US government has no interest in catching some high-profile gangsters."

They all chuckled at that, but each knew any of them could be next in the federal firing line.

"Alex, I speak for Ezra when I tell you that ever since your visit to Sing Sing, we both ensured our tax returns have been completed and that all legitimate income has been accounted for."

"That's good to know, Massimo. But remember the Feds are interested in our illegitimate money. Honest gelt earned fairly doesn't set their hearts all aflutter."

"We took advice from Meyer back in the day and stashed our spoils outside the reach of the FBI."

"For your own sakes, make sure you spread it across several jurisdictions. If you recall, Benny looked to Europe, and Switzerland is a great place to go for discreet banking, but there are places closer to home you can use too."

"Like the Bahamas?"

"Exactly, Ezra."

"We've already got that covered."

He winked at Massimo and Alex let out a sigh of relief.

"First, of course, I hope you never need to find out how watertight your plans are. Second, how sure are you there are no chinks in your financial armor?"

"Alex, I understand you have your concerns, especially because of all that you went through, but Lansky helped set us up with a load of help from Benny."

Ezra looked Alex square in the eyes to convince him his worries were misplaced. Alex smiled.

"If you got advice from Benny about how to hide your money, then you've been informed by the best."

They all laughed at this comment, in memory of the man who created the Las Vegas which had fed their wallets since the 1940s, and the Flamingo Hotel was relaunched. The same fella who was killed when he skimmed from the hotel before it had even been built. Alex recalled the moment when his sniper rifle recoiled and the first bullet ripped through his friend Benny's body.

With smiles on everybody's faces, Alex suggested they take a break and head out of the house and find a place to eat. Tito Vestri drove the three fellas over to the center of town, where they found an Italian restaurant. Soon, they were in a back booth with a waiter pouring them each a glass of red wine.

AFTER A LONG lunch, Tito transported them over to Alex's house and waited in the car while the men continued their business meeting.

"So I wanted to make sure that the Italian mob was still being respectful toward you fellas."

"Everything has been good until now. Are you expecting trouble, Alex?"

"Always, Ezra. It's not that anything is guaranteed to happen, but I want you to be prepared in case it does. While you might have heard this before, when I divest from Vegas, there is a strong chance others might try to take over your piece of the action, and I'll do my best to prevent that from occurring."

"But in the meantime, we should be on our guard?"

"Massimo, you understand everything. And that is why I couldn't just make a phone call. I wanted you to see the whites of my eyes and know that I mean what I say."

"As you are here, Alex, there is something else to talk about."

"And what's that, Massimo?"

"Our driver is looking to move state, and we wondered if you'd be interested in hiring him."

"Why the sudden need to leave Nevada?"

"Family troubles, Alex. Nothing more than that."

"Apart from wanting to run away, is he reliable?"

"For sure. He's been with us for many years and we trust the fella. At the same time, he needs to move and find employment with the right outfit. So the first person on our list was you."

"In that case, I'll take him on. It'd be cool to have somebody chauffeur me and Sarah around."

VESTRI DIDN'T UTTER a word from Miami International over to Alex's compound. Perhaps the irony of Alex driving his chauffeur was not lost on the Italian. When they reached their destination, Sarah welcomed him to his new home and left him alone with Alex soon after.

"Like so many of the buildings on these grounds, we haven't used this place since we arrived. So this will be yours for as long as you like, rent free. If you decide you want to live somewhere else, then that's fine, but it'll be on your dime. My sister lives three cottages down, so bear that fact in mind if you intend to party. I do not care what you get up to, provided it doesn't disturb her, myself, or Sarah, and no cop comes calling to find out what you're up to."

"Thank you, Mr. Cohen. Everything is clear and I promise you shall get no trouble from me."

"Call me Alex. One of the first orders of business will be for you to locate us a suitable automobile. My saloon is not going to be too comfortable if Sarah and I are in the back seat. You may borrow my car for today and find something appropriate. Then you can start your duties, although we will not be as busy as Ezra and Massimo."

"I will do whatever you ask of me. You have been very reasonable about my situation and I appreciate your generosity. I won't let you down."

"Let's hope you don't, Tito. There is one thing you can help me with which Massimo was vague about. Why did you need to quit Vegas so fast?"

"There was family trouble, Alex."

He blinked and waited, but Tito offered him nothing more.

"What kind of problems were you facing?"

Vestri's face remained unchanged and he glanced at the floor.

"Did it involve women, by any chance?"

Vestri shot Alex a look that could kill.

"We've all been there, Tito. There is no shame in experiencing difficulties in your personal life."

"I know, Alex. It's just what happened in Vegas remains there. I don't feel comfortable talking about it."

"Tito, I am not asking you to confide in me, but I have one question, and you must be honest with me. Are there any legal authorities seeking you out? Local cops, the Feds, anyone?"

"No. You have my word, Alex."

"It's all I want, Tito."

Alex walked back to the main house and sat on the patio, enjoying the afternoon's sun. Sarah spotted him and joined him, carrying a pot of coffee and two mugs.

"How is Tito?"

"Sarah, I am sure he'll be a fine driver. He chauffeured Ezra and Massimo around for long enough with no trouble."

"But?"

"He won't say why he had to leave in such a hurry. I extracted a promise from him it had nothing to do with the cops, which is something."

"Is it sufficient for you, Alex?"

"Now that I do not know."

They sipped their drinks until Sarah broke the silence.

"It'll be neat being driven around though, won't it?"

Alex grinned.

"You bet your life it will, hon."

5

THE PHONE RANG in the middle of the night and Alex fumbled around in the dark until he found the receiver.

"Hello?"

"We've had visitors in California."

Ezra's voice was flat, but his few words told him everything he needed to know. The cops had raided their Los Angeles warehouse.

"I'll be on the first flight out this morning. How soon will you be there, Ezra?"

"An hour before you, I'd expect."

Alex checked his watch, rolled over, and went back to sleep, but he awoke at five, knowing he had a busy day ahead of him. He called Tito and told him to be ready for an airport run in sixty minutes. Sarah was awake too with all the rumpus and he filled her in with the latest news.

"How do you figure they even knew about the warehouse?"

"That's one reason why I need to get over there, Sarah."

Alex wolfed down his breakfast, which Sarah made as the housekeeper hadn't arrived yet. By the time he had finished the last cheese blintz, Sarah had packed an overnight bag and Tito knocked on the front door.

"I'll be back in a day or two."

EZRA MET ALEX at the airport when he landed in LA, and they hired a rental to take them the quarter of a mile to the warehouse. They stopped around the corner and hopped out. Alex lit a cigarette and offered one to Ezra.

"No thanks. I'm trying to give them up."

He shrugged and inhaled the smoke deep into his lungs as he surveyed the frontage of his import/export business.

"Those aren't local cops."

"What makes you say that, Ezra?"

"Almost all of them are in our pocket and I don't recognize a single face. Those are Feds."

The two men stared at each other, and Alex glanced around the area. Warehouse twenty-seven was just one of a hundred identical buildings that littered the outskirts of LAX. What made the FBI choose that one?

Alex carried on puffing at his cigarette as he walked in the warehouse's direction, close enough to get a better view, but not so near to raise any interest from the Feds scampering in and out of the place.

There were two saloons and a truck parked by the entrance, and a stream of men hauling boxes out of the building and into the tail of the pickup.

"At this rate, we're going to be left with nothing, Alex."

"So be it. I would rather they took our assets away in the back of that vehicle than be the one they're carting off to headquarters."

Ezra nodded and Alex recalled how it felt when the doors to his cell slammed shut for the first time. He shuddered.

"What shall we do now, Alex?"

"The only thing we can do. Wait for the *verstinkener momzers* to leave and then see what damage they've done."

They continued to walk past the warehouse until they reached the corner of the block, where they turned right and halted. From this vantage point, they could see what the Feds were up to without being too obvious.

All the reasons they kept a storage facility near the airport became another form of unpleasantness while they stood and stared.

The noise of the aircraft engines overhead every few minutes was enough to drive a sane man straight to hell, and the sun beat down in this desolate industrial expanse.

An hour passed by and still the Feds filled up the vehicle with contraband.

"I forgot how much we stashed in this place, Alex."

"Me too. And these guys started before we even caught a plane over here. They're going to need a bigger truck."

Ezra laughed for a moment and then stopped himself as a second large vehicle arrived on the scene as the first one pulled away.

"We'll be here quite some time, Ezra. Why don't you go for a break someplace and come back later? There's no need for both of us to stand here. Then we can swap until the Feds have finished their dirty business."

"If you're sure, Alex."

"Take the rental and find somewhere quiet. An airport terminal might be a good place to hide in plain sight."

Ezra shook hands with Alex and trotted off the long way round to get back to the car. Meanwhile, Alex leaned against the corner of a building and stared as the Feds removed hundreds of thousands of dollars of merchandise from under his nose.

TWO SHIFTS EACH later and the fellas entered the premises. They had waited thirty minutes after the last vehicle departed the parking lot in case anyone returned, but the Feds seemed satisfied with their bounty.

Inside the warehouse, there were empty shelves and ransacked offices. Although the occasional piece of paper had been dropped on the floor, boot prints visible on a white background, the cops had taken every scrap of financial records they could find. Alex felt a weight in the pit of his stomach.

"Tell me we did what I always said and put a string of intermediaries between ourselves and any transactions relating to the contents of this warehouse."

"For sure, Alex. We never knew when, but this was inevitable. One certainty in our business is that the cops will raid us."

"There was a time when you'd take care of the Feds, same as any other cop, and they would turn to face the other way."

"Not anymore, Alex. It started when Bobby Kennedy was attorney general and has carried on ever since. You can't rely on anyone nowadays."

"Get a clean-up crew in here before the end of the day. I want this place gutted. If there is any item remaining by nightfall, then burn the joint down. When the Feds sniff around again, I need them to find ash and nothing else."

"Leave it with me."

Alex nodded and walked through the offices, hands in pockets, hoping to salvage anything worth the effort, but in vain. In the rental, he spoke to Ezra before he turned the engine over.

"For the Feds to show up means some *gonif* told them about our warehouse. We have a rat."

"We cannot be sure of that. Ever since Valachi spilled his guts, the Feds have been working many cases using what he gave them. This might be an example of that."

"Ezra, are you telling me that his testimony from seven years ago is the source of today's raid? That's a long time to be sitting on this address and doing nothing."

The lieutenant was silent for a spell, mulling over Alex's words.

"Alex, all I know is that the fella named loads of venues, and ours could have been one of them."

"Did you ever meet Valachi?"

"Nope."

"Me neither. I don't believe I've ever met the guy in my life. So how did he learn about this needle in a haystack? Did we even own it back then?"

Ezra pondered for a moment and shook his head.

"I can't recall, Alex. We acquired it sometime after the Bay of Pigs."

"Well, that narrows the timeline down."

Alex glanced at Ezra, who shrugged.

"Massimo might recall the details better than me. He was the one who found the place and managed the purchase."

"You are still clinging to a slender thread, Ezra. We have a rat in our midst and we are going to have to identify the son of a bitch."

"I EXPECTED YOU'D be gone for another day, at least."

"So did I, but Ezra volunteered to stay and mop up the mess."

"Do we know why the Feds chose our warehouse of all the places to raid?"

Alex laughed. "I didn't stop them to find out. Besides, someone must have ratted on us."

"Any idea who?"

"Now that is an excellent question, Sarah, and I do not have a clue."

"Are we missing any crew members? Perhaps somebody who couldn't be contacted in the last twenty-four hours?"

"That's a good starting point. The strange thing is that I have always made a concerted effort not to *schtupp* our people. I believe that paying over the going rate buys you loyalty."

"That is often true, Alex, but it is no guarantee. Some guys aren't satisfied until they have everything."

"Sarah, do you have anyone in mind when you tell me this?"

"Oh no. I'm only pointing out that whoever dropped a dime to the Feds was dissatisfied or scared. You don't spill your guts to the cops for the price of a cup of coffee."

"Or a rival. Somebody who wants to chisel into our Los Angeles operation."

"Alex, you're talking like there's a vast deal to be won out there. Most of our revenue came from narcotics and prostitution, which Massimo and Ezra now run. Other than that, there was warehouse twenty-seven, and we only kept that because it was close to the airport."

"And this is why I know it's personal. Someone tried to connect me to the stolen goods inside that building."

"Alex, the other possibility is that some local yokel scored some points with Hoover's boys and gave up a location which no one will lose any sleep over."

"Apart from me, Sarah."

6

THE FOLLOWING MONDAY, David and Alex sat in the Cohen offices with the usual pot of coffee on the table. Alex read the newspaper while David rifled through the business pages. He scanned one article, took a glug of his drink, and went through the same piece again, but as slow as possible without stopping. Then he put the paper back down.

"Pop, there's something I've got to tell you."

"Is everything all right with your kids?"

"Nothing like that. This is legal advice I'm trying to give you."

"My apologies. Do proceed."

"The Racketeer Influenced and Corrupt Organizations Act has come into force."

"David, is that supposed to mean something to me?"

"We talked about it last month, don't you remember?"

"I hope my expression answers your question. Don't get me wrong, I believe you provided me with information about this, but there isn't a single shred of its contents that has remained in my head."

"Shame on you, Pop. Is your memory going?"

"Don't get fresh with me, young man. Tell me again."

"It's known as the RICO Act and it will bite us in the ass. They've created this law to catch organized criminals. If it seems as though you are conspiring to commit a major crime, they'll arrest you under RICO. Receive payments from an illegal source like a casino skim? Then they can get you, even if they can't prove beyond a reasonable doubt that the money came from a skim."

"So they can arrest us for anything related to organized crime, even if they can't prove the details."

"Pretty much, Pop. Worse still, the maximum sentence is twenty years and all they have to do is to show you've been involved in two rackets in the last ten years."

"And with my record, that will not be too hard to do."

"There is a sliver of good news."

"David, don't hold it back."

"Each state will take a while to enshrine RICO into their laws, which means you have time to get your affairs in order. But make no mistake, Pop; this is inevitable and once the first couple of states do it, the rest will fall like dominos."

Alex let out a long whistle until the breath had left his lungs.

"That was the good news. The bad thing is that Mom may be implicated too."

Alex sat forward in his chair.

"Why do you say that, David?"

"You might have kept me at arm's length from your shadier deals, but I realized what you got up to in Havana, and I guess Mom worked for Meyer a while before you moved to Cuba."

"If the Feds can pin dirt on me, they might do the same to Sarah?"

"I reckon so. You can't undo the past, but you might distance yourselves from it as much as possible from this point onwards."

"What do you advise we do?"

"Shred any paperwork you possess relating to anything which you wouldn't want Esther to read. That is a sensible measure of how legal your documentation must be. Then, and I can't emphasize this too much, you must stop taking mob money, Pop."

Another sigh from Alex.

"I've been threatening to do that for a few years now."

"You've been saying it all my life, Pop."

"Sounds like this is when I need to mean it. How long before I receive a knock on the door?"

"A year, maybe two at the outside. Then you'll be fair game. California, New York, Illinois, Florida. You should bet at least one of them will be in the initial wave of states ratifying RICO into their statutes. Possibly all of them."

Alex swilled some coffee around the back of his throat and tried swallowing again. He always said that he preferred to hear bad news early. That it should travel faster than anything good, but the image of the Feds taking him to jail filled Alex with dread. And the sinking weight knotting in his stomach only got worse with the thought that Sarah could be dragged down at the same time.

"Looks like I have no choice, David."

7

WITH DAVID'S WORDS ringing in his ears, Alex set about deciding on a legitimate business to get involved with. A few weeks before he and Sarah left California, Alex bumped into Frank Sinatra, who suggested he try his hand as a filmmaker. At the time, Alex had laughed at the idea, but now he was warming to the prospect of putting together the financing for a movie.

"What do you think of me becoming a producer, Carl?"

The head of United Studios smiled and had another mouthful of his steak.

"Is that why you've flown back to California to visit me? You want an office in the studio?"

"Not quite, Carl. But I was hoping for a few pointers on how to get started. I'm thinking of a small project, to begin with, so I can get a hang of all the moving pieces in a film project and build up from there."

"Are you planning on investing yourself, or are you going to seek funding from elsewhere?"

"Carl, that is an excellent question, and the answer depends on how much we are talking. There is only so much of a fella's capital he will put at risk at any one time."

"Alex, I respect anybody prepared to invest a dime of his own money on a movie. I don't want to dissuade you from your plans, but most films fail to get a single frame shot, let alone reach completion and proceed to distribution."

"How come?"

"The money isn't found, or the talent isn't available at the right time. Or more likely, your studio gets bored and moves its interest on to something else, which looks as though it might be easier to deliver."

"Would I have to go through a Hollywood studio?"

Carl laughed out loud.

"Sorry, Alex, no disrespect intended, but you sounded more like Orson Welles than Alex Cohen just then. About everyone operates through a studio. You get a tremendous amount of support along the way and they hold a lot of sway when putting the package together if you are able to namedrop a big name."

"Like United?"

"Yes, we're not quite up there with Warner Brothers, but we still churn out enough product each year to keep our shareholders happy."

"Would you be willing to work with me, Carl?"

The studio boss fell silent and consumed two mouthfuls of his steak.

"Alex, we've known each other off and on for several years and I appreciate you flying over to speak with me, but you understand that the film business is ruthless and no one will back a guy, just because he knows him or he is connected. With no movie track record, United would be unable to put its name behind you. Nothing personal, but we won't support an unknown talent."

"That's a shame, Carl, but thank you for your honesty."

"Don't get me wrong, Alex. If you piece together an interesting commercial package, then let me be the first to receive your pitch. You would push on an open door from my perspective. In the meantime, I will give you an office to work out of in our lot, if that helps."

"That'd be mighty fine of you, Carl."

"It's what friends are for, right?"

BACK HOME, ALEX tried to decide what he should do next. There was gelt to be secured, perhaps from Meyer, and a story idea to be nurtured. Money would not be a problem; he knew enough men with cash to fund whatever project he wanted to put together. As for the narrative? He had no clue and Alex didn't mix in the proper circles that he could bump into anyone with creative thoughts, either.

"Alex, perhaps you should speak to Frank. He encouraged you to be a producer in the first place."

"Sarah, you're correct. We might have left Hollywood, but the people we met are still there. Sinatra should take my call, don't you reckon?"

"And then some, Alex. Never forget how much influence you had in that town."

"Apparently so."

That afternoon, Alex called Frank.

"I've got a favor to ask of you."

"How can I help, Alex?"

"Do you recall you suggested I become a movie producer?"

Silence on the line.

"Well, I decided to try it out, Frank."

"Good for you."

"And I was wondering if you could put me in touch with some guys with an idea who I might work with."

"What I've always liked about you, Alex, is that you are a straight talker. You never hid what you were when we did business together and you've never bothered with unnecessary small talk."

He sighed, as this sounded like another kiss-off.

"You know I own a stake in Warners, right?"

"Frank, I hadn't forgotten."

"Then any project which comes in my direction has to go through the studio. Do you want to work for us, because I could swing that at a push?"

"After all these years of running things my way, I doubt if that would create a successful working environment, you might say."

"Indeed, Alex. We don't work with independent producers, and not with one who has no track record in the business. You understand, right?"

"I get it, Frank. Is there any crumb you might see your way clear to offer me?"

"Don't be like that, Alex. I'm just telling you how things play out in Warners. That doesn't mean my help stops there."

"What do you mean?"

"Given that you've operated on a certain side of the tracks, there are opportunities that open up to you which some of us could not take."

"What does that involve, Frank?"

"I'll connect you with some local fellas I know who would benefit from a money man with your credentials."

"Frank, we are talking movies still?"

"Of course. Not every film comes out of Hollywood."

"No?"

ALEX HOPPED OVER to South Daytona to meet the new contacts that Frank had offered him. The location was a coffee shop in the city center.

"Thanks for taking the time to see me, Mort."

"Always happy to break bread with a man such as yourself."

Mort Lowry's crumpled sandy jacket sat over a pressed white shirt. Although the handshake was firm, Alex needed to wipe his palm dry afterward.

"Kind of you to say. I don't suppose Frank has told you why he felt we should have a conversation."

"Only in the broadest of terms, Alex. Assume I know nothing and you won't be too wide of the mark."

"It's simple. I want to enter the movie business. Funds are not an issue for me, and I'm looking for a project to put together."

Mort smiled a few seconds longer so that he made Alex feel uncomfortable.

"Alex, I'm sure we can find something for you to get your teeth into."

"What sort of thing do you have in mind?"

"There are at least four packages we are looking at, and there is bound to be one that will interest you."

"Mort, who do you mean when you say 'we'?"

"I maintain associates with whom I operate, but you don't need to worry about them. I am the only person you will meet. Let's focus on the projects themselves for now."

ALEX SAT BY the pool with a whiskey in his hand. Sarah bustled inside and joined him after a few minutes, holding a vodka tonic.

"How have you got on, Alex?"

"All right so far. Frank put me in touch with a local guy who is prepared to connect me to a film director in need of financing."

"That sounds positive."

"It is, hon."

"Then why are you looking so glum?"

"I'm not confident Mort Lowry is the right kind of fella."

"What do you mean?"

"I'm not sure yet, but there is something about him I don't trust."

"Doesn't that just make him a member of the human race?"

"You are cruel, Sarah."

She laughed out loud.

"Is there anything you have on this Mort beyond your gut feel?"

"Not yet, although I'll be doing a background check on him before we meet again."

"This is part of our move away from illegal businesses, isn't it?"

"Of course, Sarah. A couple of years ago, you asked me if I would get bored if I retired, and you were right. Films are a great moneymaking opportunity while having some fun along the way."

"In that case, why isn't Frank's recommendation good enough for you?"

"I trust Sinatra, if only because he continues to live in the shadow of Sam Giancana, whether he wants to or not. That doesn't mean that he understands how I want to behave in the future, as he has only seen me associated with the mob."

"All I ask is that you take care of yourself, Alex."

"You and me both."

8

ALEX AND SARAH popped over to visit David and Dorit, along with their two kids, for the weekly get-together. The women were with Nathan and Jojo, while Alex and David remained in the living room.

"This is a nice place you've got here, David."

"Thanks, Pop. The children each have their own bedroom and there's space out in the yard for them to run around in safety."

Alex eyed the decor and noticed the depth of the pile in the carpet and the exquisite paintings on the walls. He smiled.

"What's amused you, Pop?"

"Nothing, son. I'm pleased you are doing well, given the crumbs you extract from my table."

Now it was David's turn to smile.

"We get by."

"Looks like you are doing a little better than that. You should be proud."

David's cheeks reddened and he picked at an invisible thread on his pants until the conversation changed tack.

"How have the kids been?"

"All good, thanks, Pop."

"Has Jojo's head cold gone?"

"Turned into a hacking cough, but she'll be fine in a few days."

Alex nodded and took a sip of his coffee.

"They bounce back fast."

Almost on cue, Jojo ran into the room, leaped onto her father's lap, gave him a hug, and dropped back to the floor. Then she smiled, sniffed, and repeated the same procedure with Alex. And without a word, she zoomed out.

"Don't slam the door!"

The wood banged into the jamb, making the loud noise David was hoping to avoid. Alex laughed.

"I'd have assumed you had already figured out that you can't control your children, David."

"Is that a comment about Jojo or me?"

"You are old enough to work out the answer to that question all by yourself."

"WHENEVER I COME back from a business trip, I forget how much fun it can be to visit the grandkids."

"Alex, you make me laugh sometimes. For years, you railed against being in the same state as your family. And now listen to yourself."

"A man can change his mind, can't he?"

Sarah smiled back at her husband and he found comfort in the warmth of that glow. A sip of coffee as the couple settled into the couch and spent the rest of the evening reading the newspaper or watching television, another domestic activity that was almost alien to Alex.

"Jojo is funny. She so wants to be like her brother, but she's too unaware of herself to understand that she is just too young."

"You're right, Sarah. I'm the eldest, so didn't go through that experience. Instead, I was the one who would fight for the right to do anything: stay up late, go out by myself."

"From what you've told me, there wasn't much fighting on that front. You did what you needed to do and held the household finances together."

"That didn't stop my mom from shouting at me when I got home in the end. What about you, Sarah?"

"I have no memories of being with my family. My earliest recollections are of hustling on the street for bread."

"You had it tough, for sure."

"We all do what we need to in order to survive. I was no different from the rest, Alex."

"We both know that's not true. You are one in a million. To live through those times and to get out in one piece."

"Alex, I've told you before that you are the reason I stopped being a *nafka*."

"Waxey Gordon was the fella who freed you."

"But only because you paid him and released me from my servitude."

Alex shrugged. Looking back, he was driven as much by jealousy as anything else; he didn't want to share Sarah with any other man, and he couldn't figure out any other way of getting that to happen. The notion never crossed his mind that he was buying Sarah in the same manner he bought a new watch.

ALEX AND SARAH sat in Moishe's living room while Alecia was next door feeding their newly arrived baby. A minute later and their grandson appeared in Alecia's arms.

"Sorry I didn't pop my head around the door, but I was busy." Alecia raised Oscar a few inches and continued to whisper. "He's gone straight to sleep."

Both grandparents walked over to mother and son and grinned. Sarah asked if she could hold him, but Alecia wasn't comfortable with that suggestion.

"When he is awake, for sure. But I've only just got him down."

Moishe left to make a drink and Alex followed him into the kitchen.

"Exciting times."

"Yes, Pop." Moishe fussed over the coffee pot. "Is it normal to feel so scared?"

A smile from Alex. "Most definitely. And it never goes away, no matter how old they get."

His son glanced over at him and nodded, a twinkle in his eye.

"We spent so much time thinking about Oscar's birth that we didn't give a moment to consider what happens next."

"You and every other parent on the planet. I am the last person who should offer advice about child rearing as I was around so little with you but allow him a routine to follow and let him know your boundaries. After that, make it up as you go along, like the rest of us."

"Do you fancy a cigarette, Pop? I'm dying for one."

Alex nodded and pulled out his pack, but Moishe walked out into their yard.

"What's this all about?"

"Alecia doesn't want me to smoke inside now that we have Oscar. It's to protect his little lungs."

Alex shrugged.

"I wouldn't say you and David suffered, but if that keeps her happy, right?"

"That's how I see it, Pop."

The men sat down on two patio chairs within easy reach of where they were standing.

"And are you keeping Alecia happy by not making your relationship legal?"

Moishe sighed.

"I thought we'd been through all this before."

"We have, son. If you and she are in a good place, then who am I to argue? Part of my job is to speculate about what happens when things aren't going so well. If anything were to happen to you, what would Oscar's legal status be? Or Alecia's?"

"Pop, don't make me laugh. It's taken you until now to worry about the law."

"I am concerned about loose ends and your relationship. Marriage binds two people together in a special way. If Alecia were to pack up and leave in the morning, what rights would you have over seeing your son?"

9

MORT LOWRY WAS a piece of work. The longer Alex spent with him, the more he compared this Florida filmmaker with a reptile. From his physical manner to the way he conducted himself, the guy was cold-blooded from whichever angle Alex tried to look at it.

"You mentioned before that there were several projects which you felt I might get involved with. Perhaps you could give me some more details about them."

The lizard tongue whipped out of Mort's mouth, latched onto a cigarette, and the gecko lips took a long drag.

"We can come to that, for sure. First, I want to know what draws you into our line of work."

Alex stopped in his tracks.

"I told you when we originally met. I have some money to invest and reckon it'd be an enjoyable way to put it to good use."

Another huge inhalation left nothing but ash on the end of the cigarette.

"I get that, but why not go to United Studios? If Carl is prepared to take your call, you are pretty much made."

"Let's say that some of my past activities make it difficult for Carl to welcome me with open arms inside his studio."

"Were children involved?"

"What? No!" Mort's mind was sick. "For some of my business ventures, I became entangled with law enforcement."

Lowry eased back in his seat in the same South Daytona restaurant where they had met before. By the manner with which the waitress acknowledged Mort, this was his office in all but name, which reminded Alex of his days spent at the rear of Lindy's in New York before Dewey crashed into his life.

"Alex, you understand I do not judge, but I need to know what kind of a man I am dealing with."

"Mort, I would imagine by the time we first sat in this diner that your due diligence on me was complete and satisfactory. If not, why are we even talking?"

"No disrespect was intended, Alex. Of course, your reputation precedes you, but what you are like as a person is not always visible when people talk of legends."

"There's no need to blow smoke up my ass, Mort. I have done well, but I am not the stuff of myths. I'm only a fella trying to make a buck."

"Your modesty is becoming. All I'm saying is that in my line of work, I have little concern about what you do behind closed doors, but I need to know that you are doing it. I don't judge like I said."

Alex sipped his coffee to calm down. He ground his molars and counted to ten. Then he took another glug of his drink and lit a cigarette.

"Mort, I understand your desire to ensure that the vice squad doesn't pay a visit, and I assure you that there are no flies on me."

"Thank you, Alex. You would be surprised how many men get offended when I ask such questions, but in our business, there is no such thing as being too careful. My associates would not be impressed if I embroiled them in anything unsavory."

"And who are these guys?"

Mort stared at Alex with a blank expression.

"They are nobody you need to concern yourself with."

"Mort, over the years, I have found that deals go without a hitch if everyone involved in a project knows everybody else. If you've seen the whites of everyone's eyes, a fella will consider twice before welching on an agreement."

"I agree with you, but my partners don't appreciate me throwing their names around all over the place."

Alex inhaled his cigarette until the smoke was deep inside his lungs.

"Mort, I do not intend to broadcast their identities so anyone who walks past this diner can find out. I am asking who you want me to go into business with. That's all."

"Alex, I mean you no disrespect. Perhaps when we are working together on a particular project, the time will be right, but not until then."

HALLEL RIDLEY WAS recommended by Mort, who gave Alex the impression that he knew everyone in the film industry if they were based in Florida. At least Hallel had an office in a building, although you'd be hard pressed to notice the existence of his business premises. They were buried at the far end of an industrial park on the outer edge of Fort Lauderdale. To reinforce Ridley's desire for anonymity, the nameplate was missing from the frontage and Alex was forced to rely on the rusty number instead.

The room in which they sat was nothing to write home about. Hallel had a desk and a couple of chairs, along with a filing cabinet as far away from the doorway as possible. If he didn't know better, he'd have thought the furniture and door had had an argument. As his secretary sashayed out, having deposited two mugs of coffee, Alex broke the silence.

"You must be doing well."

Hallel nodded.

"Business has been good the last couple of years, so I indulge myself with an assistant."

Alex smiled at Ridley but doubted that the young lady had been selected for the secretarial role just because of her typing speed.

"And it is business that brings me here, Hallel."

"Mort told me you'd be calling."

"This is my situation. I intend to produce a movie here in Florida and I am looking for a lab to develop my film. And the first name that Mort mentioned was yours."

"No need to flatter me, Alex. Mort and I go back a long way. Even if I was the fifth person on the list, I wouldn't mind. That you are in my office means there is an opportunity for us to work together, and that is all I care about."

"If our business relationship grows, you will find I am not in the habit of saying things to make people feel good about themselves. So, like I said, you were the first."

Alex lit a cigarette and took a sip from his coffee. It had rested on the hotplate too long, but he knew better than to spit it back into the mug. The secretary's skills lay outside of making a hot drink for a guest, although Ridley didn't seem to mind the flavor.

"How are you funding your project, Alex?"

"I have some assets myself, and if that proves insufficient, I know enough people who'd be interested in getting involved that anything is possible. You can take it from me that money is not an issue."

"A man who doesn't worry about gelt is quite a fella in my book."

"Kind of you to say, Hallel. I have spent most of my life working hard to put food on my family's table and still have spare change to set aside for a rainy day."

"The storm is approaching and you want to make a movie?"

"Pretty much."

"Then let me show you around our facility before we get down to brass tacks."

HALLEL WALKED ALEX around the plant, and he pretended to care about the machinery he was looking at. Ridley spoke at length about how he turned the cans that Alex would supply into something that could be shown on a movie projector. The place reeked of chemicals as far as Alex was concerned and he made a mental note to suggest a different venue were they to meet again.

"Alex, earlier you didn't say when you expected to have the film ready for processing."

"That's because I haven't started production yet, but I want to know I have everything in place so that it'll be plain sailing from the moment we push the button on the project."

"Most producers I've met prefer to get the cameras rolling as soon as possible. There's nothing like the joy of watching actors on set doing their stuff."

"Hallel, I mean no disrespect to anybody in this industry, but I am not a big fan of the movies. I watch the occasional Western, but that is about it. This is a profit-making enterprise for me and nothing more. So, once all the pieces of the jigsaw fit, I will start, but not before."

Ridley grinned.

"I'm glad that you intend to take your work so seriously. Sorry, Alex, but Westerns aren't the sort of film I bring back to my pad to view, if you get my meaning?"

Alex stared blankly at Hallel, who continued to smile with a knowing expression. After three or four seconds, he stopped.

"These movies are for home use, right? You're not thinking about anything feature-length for a picture house?"

Now it was Alex's turn to be nonplussed. He had assumed Mort's projects were intended for cinemas, but some things the snake had said made little sense until now.

"Hallel, forgive the naïve question, but what films are made for home projection?"

10

"I NEED YOU to explain to me more about the projects you've got lined up for me, Mort."

Alex and the distributor were sitting in Lowry's makeshift office with coffee and cheesecake in front of them.

"What's to tell, Alex? Each will come in at under one hundred grand to make and who knows how much we can generate from them."

"When I spoke with Hallel, he talked about home movies."

"That's the main distribution model, yes. What did you assume was going to happen?"

"I was operating under the mistaken belief that they would be shown in cinemas."

A laugh from Mort. "Alex, the world is not yet ready for our films to be presented in the picture houses of this country."

Alex's mind whirred. All his conversations with United Studios had involved distribution to cinemas. That was the Hollywood model. When Carl passed him onto Mort, he had made the mistake of thinking he was going local and not into some other business altogether.

"Why can't the films be shown in the cinema, Mort?"

Another laugh, which turned into a chortle.

"There are federal and state laws that prevent us from sharing our art with a wide audience."

The man left Alex to reflect on the implications of what he had said. A short while later and a light bulb pinged on above Alex's head.

"Dirty movies."

"I expect you'll get along better with everyone in this industry if you refer to the product as adult entertainment. Actors, in particular, can be very sensitive, you will find."

Cogs spun in Alex's mind. Was this still something he should do?

"Tell me how much the authorities poke their noses in our business."

"Right now, Alex, everything is cool. We grease the wheels enough that the local cops stay off our backs and we rely on the Feds having bigger fish to catch than a small outfit in Fort Lauderdale."

"Mort, what is most important to me is not whether the content contains bare flesh, but that the authorities will deem the production of such material as an illegal act. Will it be legal to make the film?"

"I'm no lawyer, but the line blurs when we talk about the distribution, not the manufacture, of the product. Provided the scenes are filmed on private property involving consenting adults, the cops can do nothing. When we sell them to customers and ship the reels around the state, that is when a crime might be committed."

"But the risk is on you because you will carry out the transportation and delivery of the films, Mort, right? I am just the producer."

"I handle the distribution, but the images themselves can be illegal to possess, depending on what kind of film you make. The labs are key, which is why I put you in touch with Hallel. And, Alex, with all due respect, if the cops haul me in, then you should expect a knock on your door too because we are in this together."

"And Ridley too. How often do the flatfeet come calling?"

"I haven't received a visit in the last five years. As I said before, they've got better ways to fill their quota."

"And how many times have the producers you work with been interviewed by the cops?"

"It's the same answer, Alex. We pay insurance to make sure that they keep their noses out of our business."

"What about Hallel? How often does he face scrutiny?"

"Once a year, but vice never gets further than the front door. They haven't taken away a single reel of film since I've known the fella."

"And you mentioned insurance?"

Lowry glanced to his left and right, then he nodded and Alex understood.

AFTER HE EXITED the restaurant, Alex wandered back to his car, where Tito was waiting for him.

"All good, Alex?"

"Let's go home."

On the way, Alex reflected on Sam Giancana, the mob boss in charge of Florida, who had warned him after his last unauthorized hit not to get involved in any gang activities again. If he wanted his family to remain alive.

That conversation had been two years ago, and Alex considered the possibility that Sam's concerns had waned in the intervening time. If Alex was wrong, then the last thing he should do is to become a porn film producer. Why hadn't Carl Newman explained what he was getting Alex involved with when he introduced him to Lowry?

"How're your meetings going?"

"Sarah, Carl has landed me in a very different world to Hollywood."

"What do you mean?"

"Mort Lowry makes home movies, and it's taken me until today to realize this."

His wife stared at Alex like he was from another planet.

"The reason that Mort is so careful with the people he works with is because he distributes skin flicks."

Sarah blinked twice and sat down in a nearby living room chair.

"That sounds as far from legal as you might get, Alex."

"Shooting the movie is fine, providing we use consenting adults. Processing the rushes might be problematic, depending on what we capture on film. And distributing anything which shouldn't have gone through a lab is off limits too."

"Wasn't the plan for you to leave illegal activities behind you?"

"Mort distributes, Hallel processes, and I produce. They are in the firing line before me. If I am careful, then I can create plausible deniability."

"Do you believe that for real, Alex?"

He squinted and stared into his lap.

"Only one successful short generates a lot of gelt, Sarah. It would finance us throughout our retirement, so there would be a tidy nest egg to pass on to the kids and grandchildren."

"That might well be, but that won't help you if they put you in jail."

"I wouldn't let that happen, Sarah."

"And how do you imagine you'd be able to stop the cops?"

"I may not have spoken to him since Bobby Kennedy died, but I can still whisper in the ear of Sam Giancana. While he is alive, I maintain leverage with him. That means he would pull out all the stops to keep me in clover."

THAT EVENING, ALEX lay on a lounger on the patio while Sarah swam a few lengths in front of him. Thinking back, Carl had been mighty generous to offer him office space in United's studios given the kinds of films he knew he was sending Alex into head first.

The thing that worried him more than the legality of the entire venture was Mort's associates. The man's reticence to name his business partners showed their anonymity was important, and that was a cause for concern. Only criminals wanted to keep their names out of the papers, although with skin films, Alex might instead be dealing with rich men holding high office in government or otherwise engaged in the public's eye.

A sprinkle of water landed by his feet and Sarah hovered into his field of vision, bobbing at the side of the pool.

"Penny for your thoughts."

"I'm focusing my mind on porn."

She laughed.

"So long as you are concentrating on matters of business, then I don't care."

"You were concerned earlier this afternoon about the Feds carting me to prison."

"Alex, what you said about Sam makes sense. He knows what you did for the Kennedys and there is no way he can forget that, no matter how unhappy the mob might have been about you carrying out an unauthorized hit."

Sarah pushed off from the pool wall and used backstroke until she reached the other side. Then she climbed out and walked over to the diving board and hopped straight back in.

Alex considered Mort's associates again. Would the man have convinced legitimate businessmen to invest in his movies? Unlikely, but Alex had still to meet a legitimate politician, so that left the door wide open for the sort that Mort had captured in his net.

After a sip of a Scotch, Alex acknowledged what he had known deep down since Mort sidestepped the question when they first met. The investors were dubious characters, and the chances were that they were with the mob. The amount of investment capital would prevent virtually any local hood from the get-go.

By now, Sarah was out of the pool and had wrapped an enormous towel around herself while she dripped a few feet away from Alex.

"You still thinking about your adult films?"

"Almost, Sarah. Mort's associates are a concern. His reticence to name them and the circumstances of the movies makes me believe they're likely to be mob fellas."

"Tread carefully, Alex. Sam was clear that you shouldn't be in the same room as our Italian friends. Your life depends upon it."

"And yours, the kids, and the rest of the family."

11

ALEX SAT BY the pool on Meyer Lansky's patio, a place he'd been countless times over the years. His old friend sipped a mug of coffee while Alex smoked a cigarette.

"You've lived in this house for a long time, Meyer. Have you ever considered moving?"

Meyer's wife, Thelma, appeared and offered the men something to eat, but Alex declined.

"Thanks, but I ate lunch only an hour ago."

"There is cheesecake…"

She lingered on the last word, knowing how much he enjoyed a slice of the best from Lindy's restaurant.

"If you put it that way, then yes please, Thelma."

She grinned and headed to the kitchen.

"You still get New York deliveries, Meyer?"

"After all these years, a man gets used to his creature comforts. What's not to like?"

"Oh, I think it's great that you do. Why else do you reckon I visit?"

Both men beamed and stared at the shimmering lights reflected in the pool water.

"Alex, remember that I won't be here forever though."

"Don't talk like that, Meyer. You've got many years to look forward to."

Meyer turned his head to face Alex, then raised his eyes to heaven for an instant.

"For a smart man, Alex, you can be a fool sometimes. What I meant was that I am going to move to Israel under their rules of aliyah."

It was Alex's turn to stare.

"Why now? RICO?"

"Risk mitigation. I have been involved in all sorts of activities over my life and today the Feds have the power to indict me for almost any or all of them. I know you've been avoiding the mob for the last couple of years, but the days of omertà are slipping away."

"That's the glue that holds the entire machine together."

"It was, Alex. Nowadays, the Italians must contend with rats, and they are not just fleeing, but opening their mouths as they jump ship and spilling everything they know to cut down their jail time. It is a sorry world that we live in."

Alex finished his mouthful of cheesecake.

"And you are sure the Feds have you in their sights?"

"Not at all, Alex. But they will, because of who I am and what I have done. So, before I'm woken up in the middle of the night, Thelma and I shall go to the land of our fathers."

"There is also the fact that you've an automatic right of citizenship as a Jew in Israel."

"That might be a consideration for my choice of the location. Also, the weather is like Florida and at least the food will be kosher."

Alex spotted a twinkle in the corner of Meyer's eye.

"Well, you have been concerned about following the law ever since I've known you."

He cast his mind back to the days of Prohibition when they had both made their first fortunes working with Arnold Rothstein.

"When are you going, Meyer?"

"Don't stare at me with those doe eyes, Alex. I need to organize things first, but it is a matter of weeks, not months. You and Sarah should visit us."

"For sure. I'd miss you otherwise."

"If that were true, then with your record, relocate too before the Feds come knocking on your door."

OVER DINNER, ALEX told Sarah about Meyer's plans.

"Won't he miss his family?"

"Sarah, his biggest concern is that he'll end his days behind bars. Besides, his kids will visit him and the grandkids are old enough now to fly too."

"Sure, I understand why he is doing it, but I wouldn't be happy about it. You make it sound as though he is looking forward to leaving his American life."

"Meyer takes things in his stride. The man is never ecstatic nor depressed. He is a steady rock in the sea of business. So, like everything else in his life, he has accepted that this is the best course of action and is working to make it happen."

"And what about you, Alex?"

"I'm going to miss the fella, naturally. We might not sit in each other's laps, but we go back a long way and I always enjoy his company."

"We'll be able to break the habit of a lifetime and go on vacation to Israel."

"That'd be good, Sarah."

"And how concerned are you that the Feds will chase us out of the country?"

"To be fair, it is me, not you, they'd be after."

"Answer my question, Alex."

He chewed on his steak for a moment.

"If I had the choice between going to jail or living in Israel, then I'd pack my bags in the morning. I've tried Sing Sing and will not volunteer to visit again."

"So Zion is calling to you?"

ALEX TOOK ADVANTAGE of the fact that Meyer was still in the US and popped back over the following day.

"How serious are you about doing this, Meyer?"

"What on earth do you mean? I'll celebrate the New Year in Jerusalem and you can be certain of that. This is no joke or idle intention, Alex. I am fleeing this land in fear of incarceration. There is no real choice for me."

"I don't want you to go."

"There is no need for any of that. There are planes to take you to Israel if you want to use them. Besides, we will never lose what we did together in this country, even if we never see each other again as long as we both live."

Alex rubbed some moisture that formed near the corner of his right eye and swallowed hard. First Rothstein and now Lansky.

"Must everything end, Meyer?"

"Isn't it inevitable, Alex?"

"We live together, we love together, but we die alone."

"Our time is only over if we choose to make it so, Alex. Saying you can visit is no passing whim. There will be opportunities in the Middle East if we want to find them."

"Am I in danger then, Meyer?"

"What do I know? The question is not whether the Feds are investigating you today, but whether they turn their attention to you in the future."

"My affairs are all in order."

"Yet again, Alex, that is not the issue. Ask yourself if there is anyone who knows anything about any of your illegal activities. If there is the possibility of one person prepared to talk, you can bet that the Feds will put pressure on them to rat you out."

"Wouldn't it be easier for me to snuff them out instead of running away?"

Meyer smiled.

"It depends how long your hit list would be, I suppose. Every time there is a bank robbery or somebody dies in mysterious circumstances, my name appears in the papers and I am accused of being the mastermind behind the heinous crime."

"MEYER IS GOING to Israel, Sarah."

"So you said."

"I assumed he was just talking, but he means it."

"That's what you told me, Alex."

"I know, but I figured it was a play on his part, but he is serious. He's moving this month."

Alex grabbed a cigarette from the pack lying on the table by the couch while the television played in the background.

"You're going to miss him, aren't you?"

"You can bet your bottom dollar on it."

"Are you thinking of joining him in Israel, Alex?"

"Do you believe we should?"

"I asked you first."

"If Meyer is right about the Feds getting fellas to quit the mob, then it is only a matter of time before I end up in their scopes. And there is no way I am going to do another jail term. Not again and at my age."

Sarah squeezed his hand.

"Can we afford to bring the whole family with us, because I don't wish to leave them behind?"

"It's not that simple, Sarah. Before we ship our property to the other side of the world, we need to decide if we want to go there in the first place."

"But, Alex, you just said the Feds would try to take you out."

"I did, and they probably will investigate, but that doesn't mean they shall get me into a courthouse."

"Why not? What makes you special?"

"Sam Giancana will look after me. I have nothing to worry about while that man is alive. There is too much in my head that he wants to remain hidden for him not to exert all his influence on the commission if the Feds attempted to arrest me."

"You believe they would protect you, despite everything that has happened over the years?"

"Sarah, as I understand it, they'd have no choice. I wouldn't blackmail them, but they recognize the potential consequences of any conversation with a federal prosecutor."

"Would you rat them out to the commission?"

"Not for a single minute, but they can't be certain of that. The Italians in the syndicate understood how the old ways of working involved complete trust and total allegiance. The new Turks are driven by greed, not honor. When he ran things, Charlie Lucky succeeded because he respected people and held out high expectations. The commission replaced the syndicate and most of the fellas in charge forgot what made the gangs so effective."

"Are we safe here, Alex?"

"Safer than Meyer will be in Jerusalem. He'll be surrounded by Arabs who want his homeland destroyed."

12

WHILE THE PACKAGE was nowhere close to the Hollywood fodder Alex had hoped to put together, there was still sufficient profit in the project to justify taking Mort's suggestion and running with it.

One advantage that Alex offered over others in the business was that he could afford to buy a warehouse to use as a movie set instead of hiding their operation from some building landlord. And the best of Florida's adult film community wanted to get involved because they could be sure of getting a paycheck at the end of the week.

Jimi Visscher sat in Alex's production office, which he had appropriated on the west side of the Fort Lauderdale building. To make it all sound more official than he felt it was, Alex told himself that this was his film studio.

"Thank you for agreeing to meet with me, Jimi. What do you want to know about the project?"

"Mort has mentioned very little, Alex. Just that you are the money man and keen to get involved in our business."

"Not far off. This will be my first foray into the Florida movie industry, but I have lived in Hollywood for several years and have many connections there."

The corners of Jimi's lips curled upward.

"And I know what you are thinking, Jimi. If I'm so closely connected with Frank Sinatra, what am I doing making skin flicks in Florida?"

Jimi shrugged, but Alex knew he was right. That was the question he'd have asked if the roles were reversed.

"Well, the West Coast didn't agree with me and I wasn't prepared to spend the time building up a reputation when I could get a Florida production up and running in a matter of months."

"We all have our reasons, Alex, for our involvement in adult entertainment. Nobody judges."

"What about yourself, Jimi?"

"I am an artist. I am in love with the female form in all its guises."

Alex raised an eyebrow and Jimi released a roar of a laugh.

"Sorry, Alex. I couldn't resist. Why do I direct skin flicks? Because it's easy and I get very well paid to stare at tits and ass all day."

Alex took a long drag on his cigarette and moved on to describe the idea behind the project.

"This is a story about…"

Jimi raised his palm in the air.

"Forgive me, Alex, but when there's a screenplay, I'll read it. If we turn up on the first day's shoot and there's no script to hand over to me, then I'm out of here. Over the years, I find I don't need to get bogged down in the details until they matter. No disrespect, but you are unknown in these parts. While Mort's word is good enough for me to get on board with a project, you still must prove you can put a package together. If you pay me my money on time and in full, then I'll film whatever the hell you require me to."

"Understood, Jimi. And there will be nothing illegal happening on my lot. You have my personal guarantee."

"Alex, if you wish to pay an underage girl to be banged by some stud you found, I will not call the cops or storm off set in indignation. Provided everyone acts as though they are a professional, I will do whatever you ask."

"I like a man who speaks his mind."

"We are straight talkers in the Netherlands."

"Do you know of any directors of photography you would recommend?"

Jimi sniggered.

"You moved in the Hollywood crowd, didn't you? Adult entertainment rarely spends the greenbacks on those kinds of people. I have two cameramen I'd be happy to work with and everything else we'll make up as we go along. When are you going to start casting?"

WITHIN A COUPLE of weeks, Alex had cameras, lighting, and even sound covered. Mort was putting him in touch with a set designer, costumes were being made and the only thing missing that needed to be sorted was the cast.

Jimi offered to help and put himself on a day rate for the task, which Alex didn't appreciate. He hoped the director would be more engaged in the movie, but he knew that the man was motivated by money and the sight of bare flesh.

So he agreed to the payments. If nothing else, Alex knew he could trust Jimi's judgment as it wasn't clouded by any care about the content of the film. If the actor was good, Jimi would say so and if not, then they wouldn't need to waste their time on the individual for longer than it took Jimi to utter the stock phrase "Thank you. We'll get back to you with a decision shortly."

Alex had placed advertisements in the entertainment press that covered the whole of Florida and, sure enough, on the first day of open casting, a sea of creatives flooded the studio building. Jimi had the foresight to bring a couple of girls to act as general assistants, and they organized and hustled the men and women around until everyone was sitting down and waiting to be called in.

THE TWO MEN sat behind a pair of desks, positioned so there was a large space in front of them for the actors to show off their skills. There was a table, chair, and couch in case they needed props.

Jimi pressed a button on an intercom and asked one of his assistants to send the first actor through.

The guy was tall and muscular. He handed over his resume with a mugshot attached using a paperclip.

"How many productions have you been involved in, Hank?"

"Five as lead, ten more in supporting roles, Mr. Visscher."

Jimi gave Hank a handful of pages: a section from the end of the first act. The actor read through the script in no time at all.

"Show us what you've got, Hank."

The guy nodded and, to Alex's surprise, whipped off his shirt and unbuckled the belt, holding up his jeans. Then his pants fell to the floor, and Alex didn't know which way to look. Jimi stood up and walked around the actor, staring at the guy's body from every angle.

"Thanks, Hank."

The guy nodded, put on his clothes, and left the room.

"What the hell happened there, Jimi?"

"I don't understand what you mean, Alex."

"We didn't hear him utter a single word of dialogue."

"And you expect we should judge him on his diction? I don't think so, Alex. Remember that the eyes of our audience are not focused on the leading man. Provided he has a working *schlong*, we have got little to worry about."

Alex nodded and felt the heat in his cheeks.

"But we won't be seeing Hank again. I spotted a mole on the inside of his left thigh and that will not look good in any close-up."

Jimi pressed the intercom button and another potential star walked through the door, clasping a resume and photo. One day later and Jimi was satisfied they had found their hero, as well as his nemesis. There were sufficient others who appeared right that they could use for bit parts too.

"Tomorrow we start with the leading lady."

JIMI RAN THE auditions for the actresses somewhat differently. Sure, there were resumes and photos, but this time Alex's director took much more care, even asking them to read some lines before getting them to disrobe.

"All eyes are on the woman. If we are to sustain our audience's interest over more than a few minutes, they should believe in her and, let's be honest, they must want to fuck her too."

Alex accepted Jimi's wisdom as the filmmaker seemed to know what he was doing. They went through countless women by lunchtime. None of them appeared bad to Alex, but on each occasion, Jimi thanked them for their time and promised to get back to them.

"What are you looking for, Jimi?"

"Someone with that special sparkle, you know?"

Alex shook his head because he did not know what Visscher meant at all. However, the next woman to walk through the door caught Jimi's eye, for sure. After Tess Ryder had spoken her lines for a minute, Jimi quizzed her about her background and then ordered her to disrobe.

She stood straight and still as Jimi sauntered around her. Once in a while, he would touch her shoulder and when he returned to look her directly in the eyes, he reached out and placed a hand on her chest. Then he led her to the couch and sat down with Tess on his lap.

As they necked, Alex decided to leave the room. During fifteen long minutes in the anteroom, Alex consumed two cigarettes and a large mug of coffee.

JIMI REPEATED HIS audition technique for every actress that came through the door. Three days later, Alex wondered whether Visscher was doing this only to slow down the process and earn more cash. Then Liddy Bosch appeared in the room.

Alex closed his mouth and stood up to walk around the woman, just as the director had done with all the other actresses. As he was staring at her, Jimi asked Liddy to read her lines, which she did without blinking. Once she had finished, Jimi's intuition told him to exit stage left. Alex took her by the hand and spun her around like they were in the middle of a dance. She smiled and shrugged, then removed her clothes.

He swallowed hard, as Alex never believed this moment would ever happen. Before him stood the spitting image of his beloved Rebecca, the first love of his life who caught a lethal bullet aimed at him when he was living in Vegas. He had to have her.

October 1971

13

THE SHOOTING OF Alex's first film wrapped after only three weeks, which Jimi informed him was a long schedule for adult entertainment. They waited until Easter before beginning the next project; enough time for the investment gelt to get returned in spades.

In each of the subsequent pictures, Alex ensured Liddy was in the cast. Jimi didn't mind as she was easy on the eye and happy to do whatever was asked of her.

"You are very kind to me, Alex."

"Don't mention it, Liddy. You do more for me than I could ever offer you."

They lay in bed in a suite Alex had built next to his office in the studio. It meant he could work late and start early without being forced to shlep around Florida. The other advantage was that it gave him private moments with the woman that so reminded him of Rebecca.

"Alex, you treat me with respect and ask little of our moments in the sack. For me, that is a godsend."

He reflected for a moment and shrugged. He was just an ordinary fella cheating on his wife. A hunger bore into his stomach as he reminded himself of his guilt, and an image of Sarah flashed into his mind.

"Time to go to work." He got out of bed and went to freshen up, while Liddy languished under the sheets. By the time he'd finished with the shower, she had left, so Alex was left with only the scent of their coupling as a fading memory.

THE FOLLOWING DAY, Alex took Sarah out to one of the many protected casinos in Miami-Dade. They hadn't spent an evening together outside their home for quite a while.

The food at El Rancho Florida was adequate. Although Sarah enjoyed her linguine, Alex's steak was a touch too tough for his liking. Then he bought each of them a pile of chips and they walked into the gaming room.

She remained with Alex as he sauntered from the roulette wheels, over to the blackjack, and then off to the poker tables. Sarah had little interest in seven-card stud, so she moved back to the wheels of fortune, where she whiled away some time without having to get too engaged with the game itself. She played a simple bet on red, then black, and to break the monotony, every few minutes, she would pick a new lucky number.

Half an hour later and somehow she had broken even, although she couldn't explain any strategy she might have used. She exited the game and sauntered among the tables until she spotted an empty seat at a blackjack station.

This time, after fifteen minutes, she was in profit by several thousand and quit while she was ahead. Then she picked her way around the room until she ended up standing behind Alex, who was engrossed in his hand. When it was over, she tapped him on the shoulder.

"Shall we break for a drink?"

He blinked and agreed, thanking those at the table before he took his considerable winnings away with him.

"How did you do, Alex?"

"Well, thanks. You?"

"In profit for once."

He nodded his appreciation but had nothing to add. For a second, an image of Liddy's smile flitted across his mind and his cheeks warmed with the guilt of what he had been getting up to over the past year.

They sat at a bar off to one side of the main area, and a waitress arrived to take their order. As she walked off, someone or something caught Alex's eye at a table on the other end of the row of tables.

"I'll be back."

With that, he lit a cigarette and left Sarah on her own as he strode over to a man hugging a vodka tonic.

"If I didn't know any better, I'd say you followed me here, Richard."

The fella glanced up as Alex spoke, recognition flowing across his face.

"Join me, Alex?"

"I was going to make the same offer to you. My wife is just over there." He pointed in Sarah's direction, and the guy nodded and brought his drink over.

"Sarah, let me introduce you to Richard Cain."

"Pleased to meet you."

The two men sat down and Alex picked up the Scotch which had been delivered to the table in his absence. A clink of glasses and they made a toast to wealth and happiness. Richard's idea.

"How have you been, Richard? I don't believe we've bumped into each other since our last trip to Mexico."

A lightbulb switched on above Sarah's head as she pieced together where she had seen the fella's face before.

"How is Sam?"

"I DIDN'T KNOW you were so fond of games of chance, Richard."

"There's nothing wrong with an occasional visit to a casino if I'm not there on business."

"Richard, do you manage Giancana's gaming interests in Florida?"

Sam's capo pretended not to hear Sarah's question, but it was well placed.

"Is Sam likely to return to the US soon?"

"Not right now. Matters are quite complex, but he doesn't feel ready to face the heat at present."

Alex left that answer alone as Richard was being evasive. That was two inquiries he had slammed into the long grass.

"Do you prefer cards or dice?"

Sarah made another attempt to start a conversation with Sam's henchman. He shrugged.

"I don't care for either."

"So you'd rather be at a roulette wheel."

No noticeable response.

"You fellas enjoy your chat. I'm going back to win me some more cash at blackjack."

After Sarah wandered off, Richard showed the waitress that he wanted another refreshment by raising his empty glass in her general direction.

"Your wife talks too much, Alex."

"She was being polite, Richard. She is not responsible for the fact you refused to answer her questions."

Cain nodded and waited for his drink to arrive.

"Whatever. I didn't come here to make small talk with an ex whore."

"Watch yourself, Richard."

"My apologies, Alex. I meant no disrespect to you."

"Accepted. I assumed you were here to place a bet?"

"No, Alex. That is what you two told me I was doing in this joint."

"So it is no accident that we bumped into each other?"

Cain smiled for a second.

"You could put it that way. I'm here to offer you a friendly reminder from Sam."

"And what does Giancana wish me to remember?"

"Everything that he told you in '68. He is the only member of the commission who didn't demand you were hit back then. What happened was between him and you, but he wanted you to bear that fact in mind as you pursue your business ventures."

Sam had omitted to inform Cain that Alex had organized the assassination of Bobby Kennedy, which protected the Italian mob from his ongoing assaults on them, but it was an unauthorized hit. Without Giancana's protection, he would have been dead within a week of Kennedy's flatlining.

"Thanks to Sam's advice, I have been seeking to extricate myself from any dealings which are illicit."

"Fine words, Alex, but that's not true, now is it?"

"What do you mean?"

Richard peered into Alex's eyes, not sure if Alex was being naïve or very coy.

"We know you have worked hard to distance yourself from anyone with connections and Sam appreciates that. He really does, but you have not been careful enough in all your enterprises."

"I suppose you are here to tell me what I am doing wrong, Richard?"

"In a way, Alex. Have you thought how the film industry can operate in this state?"

Now it was Alex's turn to stare at Cain.

"I had not considered the possibility that the mob was involved. My aim has been to involve myself with local independent operators only."

Richard laughed.

"You forget an octopus can have its tentacles in many places at the same time, Alex. Did you believe that film processing and distribution could take place and not have Sam dip his beak into the affair?"

"None of that is illegal, so I couldn't find an angle for you fellas."

"When those moving images are transported around the country, then many cops need palms greased to get that to happen without too much friction."

"I hope you understand that there was no disrespect intended on my part toward Sam on this matter. I believed I was following his instructions to the letter. Now I know otherwise."

"We are both businessmen and Sam has made money out of your cinematic efforts. I have no idea why, but he still wishes to protect you. To be honest, I advised him to cut all his ties with you a long time ago, but he has paid no heed to my suggestion."

Alex knew the reason Giancana continued to support him even now was what he knew about the Italian's past and his involvement with the Kennedy clan. And if Sam had chosen not to divulge that to Cain, there was no way Alex felt the need to share this in the middle of a casino bar.

14

ALEX SIPPED A coffee while his sons settled down in the family offices. He lit a cigarette and waited for the two men to sit at the table and compose themselves.

"Thank you for taking the time to see me today. There is important business to discuss."

David's eyes flitted at Moishe, who in turn glanced back at his brother. Neither had a clue what was happening and that was the equal playing field that their father wanted.

"The hour has come for us to talk about the Trans-American Wire Service."

"I am amazed that it's still running."

Alex stared at David for a second.

"Just because it is old doesn't mean that we should consign it to the trash can."

"That wasn't my point, Pop. I meant that with all the new technology at our disposal, I am surprised there are bookies still relying on our wire service to get track results from around the country."

"David, you forget that most illegal operations have few options available to them, which is one way that we remained in the game all these years."

Alex took a deep drag on his cigarette and recalled the initial year of its operation. They were hard times.

"How long has it been running?"

"Since before the Flamingo opened its doors. The first couple of years we competed against a rival service, but before Benny Siegel met his maker, we had secured a monopoly across the country."

"We, Pop?"

"Myself, the usual Vegas interests and some Italian friends."

Another glance between Moishe and David.

"Stop looking at each other that way. The Trans-American is, and always has been, a legitimate venture. Some of our customers are involved in off-track betting without a permit, but that is not our concern. We possess legal contracts with them and they pay for a service rendered."

"And how does all that fit in with your Italian friends?"

"Moishe, they provided investment capital when I was cash poor and it was kept off the books. There are no records of those transactions and, therefore, they did not occur. The current directors of the business are your mother and me."

"And do you use it as income, because I don't believe I've heard either of you mention it all these years?"

"You are right, David, that it doesn't get much airspace, but it is a fine generator of gelt into the family. The funny thing is that this enterprise has a swathe of employees across the country and is doubtless the most conspicuous of all the businesses I hold a stake in."

"Visible isn't the same as high profile, Pop. The casinos are far better known by Joe Public."

"Indeed, but I divested my direct interests in all the Vegas gaming houses over the last couple of years, Moishe."

"And you've done all of this behind our backs?"

"Son, you understand as well as I do that there are some things best left unknown to you and David. Any secrecy entailed is to protect you from any downstream impact."

"You mean what we don't know can't be reported to the Feds?"

"Close. What you don't know can't hurt you and no cop can accuse you of hiding the truth from them. Ignorance is a marvelous defense."

"And we are wallowing in it in spades, Pop."

Alex nodded at Moishe, although he wasn't sure of the intent behind his son's words. Another drag on his cigarette.

"So, where does that leave us?"

"Simple, David. The time has come for me to hand the organization over to you two. The plan is that Sarah and I will step aside as soon as your names are on the shareholder register."

"How much is the business worth?"

"Several million."

David whistled.

"I can't speak for Moishe, but I don't have the money to acquire a majority stake in a multi-million dollar enterprise. And that's no joke."

"I will make each of you a personal loan of whatever amount Moishe's evaluation dictates the company is worth. That way, you get the money to purchase the stock, we record the correct amount in the books and I can then carry out an appropriate withdrawal. You both work out the details so that these transactions are legal, although I would appreciate it if we minimized the volume of paperwork that needs to be generated."

Now it was his sons' turn to gulp down a slug of coffee at the news. David surfaced before Moishe.

"Will one of us get a larger stake than the other?"

Alex smiled at the potential for sibling rivalry in these middle-aged men.

"We shall ensure that you have an equal interest and, for the first year, Sarah retains a two percent stake and a voice on the board, just in case you guys find it hard to agree on all matters relating to the company. She has a casting vote in the event of any deadlock, but after twelve months, she will sell that share, splitting it between you so you end up as fifty-fifty partners."

ALEX HOPPED OVER to Palm Springs the next day to meet with Ezra and Massimo. There was news to broadcast but he was expecting a less than enthusiastic response, and he wasn't disappointed.

"I am divesting my interests in the Trans-American Wire Service."

"After all these years? Why now?"

"Ezra, I still need to reduce my exposure to some of my business ventures. It is time."

"But what will happen to us?"

"Ezra, whatever may occur, I always look after my friends and close associates. Sarah and I will not leave you fellas high and dry; far from it. Instead, we shall hire you as consultants to the venture with an annual fee in line with your current revenues."

"This is generous of you, Alex."

"Massimo, it is what you deserve. Until now, I paid you out of my earnings and we've all been satisfied with that situation. But I want you to know that your future earning potential is protected, even when Sarah and I leave the scene."

"Who are you selling it to, Alex?"

"David and Moishe are taking over the business. We keep it in the family."

"And what will your backers make of this upheaval?"

"They won't care. It is a nice little income generator for them, but nothing more. Provided the wheels don't fall off the bus, they won't pay attention to who's driving the thing."

Massimo nodded because what Alex said made sense. The mob needed Trans-American in the '40s when they had no other way of rigging bets from the Eastern Seaboard and out to California. Now, it trotted along, but would never raise any eyebrows.

"Will we still be expected to crack heads when the need arises?"

"Ezra, your consultancy services relate to new transactions and client relations. How you maintain the customer base and generate fresh sales is not for me to say."

Alex winked, and they all got the joke. There were so many bodies buried in the Mojave desert, you'd be surprised there was sufficient sand to cover all the corpses.

"And that means we'll earn less over time if we take inflation into account."

"I am impressed, Ezra. You sound more like an accountant than ever before. Do not get bogged down in the details. We shall do right by you at all times. David will draw up the contracts and include any terms you consider are appropriate, such as an annual percentage increase to your fee."

His lieutenant nodded and fell silent.

"Do your sons have any plans for Trans-American?"

"No, Massimo. I doubt if David and Moishe had any time to think about it. I only told them yesterday and then hightailed it here to tell you fellas what was happening."

"It'll be strange for you not to be at the helm."

"Kind of you to say so, but much has happened since we toured the country, busting chops to build the wire network and convince bookies to buy our service against their will. A man has played golf on the moon, for goodness' sake, and I haven't even bothered doing that on Earth."

ONCE THE INK was dry on the shareholder documents, David asked Alex to head over to the family office. Moishe was there too, although Alex wasn't all that surprised.

"We've got some news for you, Pop."

"Is there time to pour myself a drink before you tell me?"

"Sure thing, Pop. Sorry."

Alex sat down, sipped his coffee, and lit a cigarette, as he always did when it was the point in the day to talk business.

"Moishe and I will dispose of the Trans-American Wire Service. It is not something we have much interest in, either of us, and its past is tied too closely to illicit activities. So we want no part of it."

"Have you informed Massimo and Ezra of your plans?"

"Not yet, Pop. We wanted you to be the first to know."

"I appreciate the respect you are showing me, but your fellow shareholder should be in this room. Where's Sarah?"

"Pop, we told her this morning. We aren't conspiring to remove the company from under her feet."

"Pleased to hear it. What will you do with the proceeds?"

"Nothing specific yet, but we'll plow the gelt into other investments after you receive a ten percent gift from us."

"There is no need, Moishe."

"Yes, there is, Pop. You made Trans-American what it is today and deserve to reap the rewards."

"Understood. May I make one suggestion?"

"What?"

"Don't sound so concerned, David. All I was going to say is that you should visit Las Vegas and tell Ezra and Massimo to their faces what for them will be bad news. Nobody wants to be told they've been dumped by phone."

15

ALEX DROVE HOME from the Fort Lauderdale studio and arrived in time to see Sarah sitting by the pool, soaking in the afternoon rays.

"I'm surprised you're back so soon, Alex."

His cheeks reddened as he recalled the lunch break spent with Liddy in his makeshift suite.

"There's no reason to be. I live and work here, after all."

"Sometimes you do. That much is true."

"What are you saying, Sarah?"

"Do you want to do this now, Alex? I'm happy to have the conversation, but I doubt whether you are ready for it."

"I've no idea what you are talking about."

"Alex, your ability to lie to men is unbridled, but you are lousy at lying to me. We both learned this many years ago."

Sarah reached out and took a sip of her red wine. Then she lit a cigarette and waited for Alex's response.

"I was on the film set and now I am back home. I want to work through how to handle Ezra and Massimo as the boys are selling off Trans-American."

Sarah sighed.

"All that is true, Alex, but you are lying by omission. We both know what has been going on this past year. I remained silent until now because I figured you've been good to your word ever since we got back together. Besides, one indiscretion does not make you a bad person. It's just a shame that she's another actress."

He slumped down with the weight of her words and stared at his wife. She was so hard to read.

"There are many actresses in the film. Do you believe I am schtupping all of them?"

"Don't be ridiculous, Alex. You are far too old to have that much stamina, and I should know."

His cheeks glowed.

"There's going to be one. Who she is doesn't matter to me as much as the fact that she exists at all, and you couldn't even be bothered to deny it. Before our divorce, you had the decency to pretend. Do you hold me in such low regard, Alex?"

"Not at all, Sarah. I love you."

His voice trailed off, as he had no idea what to say. How could he explain that the only reason he was attracted to Liddy was because of her resemblance to Rebecca? Besides, she was right; he was no good at lying to her.

"You *farbissener* momzer."

"What do you want us to do, Sarah?"

"No clue. I wasn't expecting you to admit it. Even now, you're able to surprise me."

"I possess hidden shallows."

"Do you intend to stop?"

"I can try. I mean, yes."

"Does she hold any importance to you as a person, or is it just how she looks?"

Alex smiled.

"She is twenty years old with a porn star body and I am flattered she'll share her bed with me. Liddy spends her time off set taking drugs and lounging around. What you see is all you get."

"We live together, we love together, but we die alone."

"I understand, Sarah. I'll do whatever you wish because despite my behavior, I love you and I am at the point in my life where I know that the last thing I want is to die a lonely old man."

Another sip of her wine and Alex lit a cigarette.

"If you need to carry on having sex with this woman, then go ahead. It is not as though we don't have our own intimate moments. But I can't say I forgive you at this point, because you've hurt me and this isn't the first time, now is it?"

Alex shook his head and cast his eyes down to the ground. He didn't deserve this woman.

"Thank you."

"I should make you get out of the business altogether. That would be a fitting punishment, but it's a good moneymaker, isn't it?"

"Yes, sex sells."

Sarah smirked.

"You don't need to tell me that, baby."

A blink and Alex recalled their first months together, Sarah a Bowery nafka, and Alex in charge of a local gang. He paid for her time because that was the only way they could be together. Then he stopped paying, and she continued to welcome him into her bed.

"I've run enough prostitution rings to know the truth of that too, Sarah."

"HOW ARE YOU progressing with your sale of the family jewels?"

"Don't be like that, Pop. When you gave Moishe and I control, you knew there was a possibility we would divest."

"I was just giving you a hard time, David. Both your mother and I support your decision, even if we disagree with it."

"Pop, if you stood back for a second and examined the business with fresh eyes, you would be staring at a dying shark. Sure, it generates a positive income now, but there is nowhere for it to go but to the bottom of the sea. We televise races and beam them into people's homes across this vast country."

Alex nodded because he knew David was right. He had given his sons a dead weight, and the good thing was that they had the sense to get rid of it before it became a noose around their necks.

"And how did Ezra and Massimo react when you gave them the news?"

"Unimpressed. Their biggest concern was to ensure their consultancy contracts were signed before the sale."

"They dipped their beaks in that trough too, you know."

"We understand that, but they didn't blink between being told we were selling and wanting to feather their own nests."

"You must be cold in business and not let emotions impede an opportunity."

"Is that how you've played it over the years?"

"As well as I am able. The only times I've found myself in trouble was when I forgot that or when fellas got in my way."

David's wife Dorit appeared and offered Alex a mug of coffee. Jojo and Nathan stormed through with no acknowledgment of the men's presence.

"Glad to find the grandkids are full of high spirits."

"Never a dull moment around here."

The door slammed shut and the thud of the children's footsteps beat up the stairs.

"Where were we?"

"Trans-American, Pop."

"Oh yes. You'll need to be careful to make sure that Ezra and Massimo don't feel you are cutting them out of a deal. It is always best to be generous with them in the short term. They invariably pay you back with interest later on."

"Thanks for the advice, Pop, but do you imagine Moishe and I will work with those two in the future?"

"Why wouldn't you? They were excellent earners for me, ever since we were young men in the Bowery."

"That's the point; they are your people and not ours. We seek different qualities in our business partners."

"Loyalty and hard work not on your list, David?"

"I'm thinking more of their other skills relating to the less legal end of the spectrum."

"They are stand-up fellas."

"Moishe and I know that, which is why they scare us so much."

ALECIA LET ALEX into the house and showed him into the living room.

"Moishe will be back any minute now—he was expecting you."

"No matter. You go about your business and I'll wait for him."

"Alex, kind of you to say, but I was brought up with better manners than that. Can I get you a drink?"

"That'd be great."

She hustled off for a few minutes and returned with a pot of coffee and a plate of snacks. Alex smiled and took a macadamia nut and white chocolate cookie without waiting to be asked.

"There are plenty more where they came from, Alex."

"Good, because it tastes wonderful."

Alecia beamed and poured them both a coffee as he lit a cigarette and eased back into his armchair. Then he stubbed it out, remembering how she felt about smoking. He glanced down at his watch and she eyed the clock hanging on the wall behind him.

"He won't be long, Alex."

"Sure thing. How are you guys getting along?"

"Huh? Just fine, thank you. Work keeps Moishe busy and Oscar is a beautiful handful."

"He just gets bigger every time I see him. Where is he, by the way?"

"The maid took him for a walk to tire him out before lunch."

"With a bit of luck, he'll be back before I go. It's been a few weeks since he's sat on my knee."

"Soon, we'll need to reinforce your lap, Alex. The little 'un sure keeps growing."

He was about to reply when there was a rustle at the front door and Moishe shouted hello. He walked into the room and halted in his stride as he noticed his father with cookie crumbs at the corners of his mouth and a coffee on the go.

"Pop. What a pleasure."

"Now you are back, my boy, there are some details about Trans-American to run through."

16

ALEX VISITED THE studio a week later. Filming was about to wrap on his latest project and he considered it a good idea to put in an appearance in front of the crew. Despite his best intentions, he and Liddy had spent at least three nights together since he confessed his sins to Sarah.

Before he even arrived on set, there were raised voices and general unrest in the air. Alex strode over to the director's chair, which was empty. Jimi headed toward him, fire in his eyes.

"Do you know where she's got to?"

"No. Who?"

"Liddy, of course. She was due to be here by eight and I had intended on finishing the whole epic by lunchtime. Now this."

Alex twisted around and noticed that everyone was there, apart from Liddy.

"Has anyone seen her this morning, Jimi?"

"Nope. The rest of the cast went out for drinks last night and she joined them, but later said she had something to do and left by eleven."

"Did she say what she was up to?"

"You know what I know. She has vanished from the face of the earth."

"Sorry, Jimi, but has anyone gone over to her apartment?"

"First thing I did, Alex, when she was a no-show."

"And you've searched everywhere around the studio?"

"Yep. It beats the crap out of me. Do you reckon Liddy's been abducted?"

"Let's not get dramatic so soon. The chances are that she's passed out at her place and not able to answer the door."

Jimi's eyes glanced downwards.

"That's not it, Alex. Suffice to say that I made sure she wasn't hiding from me when I popped over."

Alex blinked.

"Was the door left on its hinges?"

"I used the key she hid under her doormat. No damage to the fabric of the building."

Alex shrugged.

"Then we had better sit it out and wait. Why not send the cast and crew for an early lunch? There's no point in all of us sitting and staring at a non-existent actress."

Jimi smiled. Tempers were frayed and if Liddy swanned in right now, nobody would operate at their best. Alex figured he'd go to his office and make some coffee. By the time he had chugged a mug down, he might have a better clue what to do afterward. As much as waiting was a good plan, he preferred to do something other than sit on his haunches.

Alex wandered through the set and out the other side of studio B. One hundred feet along was the next building and he popped inside to be greeted by his secretary.

"Hello, Mr. Cohen. No messages today."

"Sheila, I've sent everyone else off for an early lunch. Why don't you do the same?"

The woman needed no encouragement, grabbed her clutch bag, and hightailed it away from her desk. Alex smiled and sauntered into his office. Everything was where he had left it two days before. A pile of papers waited patiently for him to review them and a tumbler that used to contain Scotch rested on a low table. He made a note to speak with the cleaners.

Alex put on a pot of coffee and walked through to his bedroom annex. He headed straight for the bathroom and relieved himself. On the way back, he stopped in his tracks. An ankle was sticking out from the other side of the bed. A naked woman's foot.

Despite himself, Alex peered around the corner of the blankets and stared. There was Liddy, face down, with a needle sticking out of her arm. Near her ear was an upturned spoon and a pile of brown powder remained on the bedside table.

None of that caused him to flinch, even for a second. What sent a shudder down his spine was the fact that she was naked from the tip of her toes to the top of her head. Why would she have taken her clothes off before shooting up? It made no sense.

Alex blinked again and sighed, a wave of sad realization spreading through his frame. He squatted down next to his lover and closed her eyes. Then he bent down and checked under the bed. Her clothing was nowhere to be seen, which was when he understood what had happened to his Liddy.

He threw a blanket over her body and walked out to speak with Jimi.

"I've found Liddy. She's dead."

Jimi's jaw fell to the floor.

"Overdose?"

"That's what the person who killed her wants us to believe."

ALEX INSTRUCTED JIMI to leave the studio and not return until the next day. Then he called Tito and issued a variety of instructions. Within an hour, there was no trace of Liddy Bosch in Alex's makeshift sleeping quarters. The bed was made, the narcotics were no longer resting on the table, and her body had been whisked away.

He refrained from asking Tito where he was taking the corpse, but Alex was certain that no one would ever find Liddy. All he had was the memory of her scent and the touch of her flesh. That and the guilt of how he had betrayed Sarah.

As far as the film business was concerned, she had left a drinks party in the late evening and was never seen again. A vibrant career in the adult entertainment industry cut short under mysterious circumstances.

The journey home was long and the roads never seemed to run out, but after a lifetime, Alex reached the house and slunk through the front door. He walked through the building until he found himself out on the patio at the back and he stopped by the pool.

"What's the matter, Alex?"

Sarah's voice came from behind him and he swiveled around to see her on a lounger with a magazine in her hands.

"There's been a problem at the studio."

"Oh, what's happened, Alex?"

He fumbled in his pockets for a cigarette and realized this was going to be his first smoke since finding that foot sticking out on the carpeted floor.

"Liddy's dead, but that is our secret. You, me, Tito, and Jimi are the only ones to know."

Sarah put her magazine down on her lap and took a glug of her drink.

"Why is it a secret?"

"Someone killed her. They tried to make it appear as though it was an accident, but they were careful to ensure that a seasoned traveler like myself would realize it was a hit."

He stared at his wife, who took another sip of her coffee. Then she grabbed a cigarette out of her pack.

"Match me, Alex."

He walked over and lit her smoke. Then he sat down on the neighboring lounger and continued to stare.

"You know anything about it, Sarah?"

Her cheeks turned pale.

"No. Why would you say that? I…"

"If it wasn't you, and I know it wasn't me, who did for her?"

"Did you believe I murdered that girl?"

"Sarah, I have no idea. You must admit you had a motive, but no matter what has happened between us, I have never known you to go to such extreme measures."

She sighed and took a hard drag on her cigarette.

"Then who, Alex?"

He considered matters for a short while as he finished his smoke.

"She was a successful actress working at a profitable Florida studio. A rival production company, maybe?"

"Alex, the big guns in Hollywood are ruthless, but I can't imagine they'd ever do anything like that to an actress just to attack another filmmaker."

"It sounds farfetched, Sarah. So that leaves the mob or local gangs. Or someone close to me who wants me to pay attention to the world beyond Florida films."

"A mob hit?"

"Why not? They left her face down on the floor with her vein opened oozing blood."

A wave of grief engulfed him but he knew that Sarah did not deserve for him to behave this way in front of her. He got up and scurried over to the summerhouse to avoid her sight.

A minute later, she appeared at the door and joined him. She came over and put an arm around Alex's shoulders as he sat and sobbed.

"She might have tried to take you away from me, but nobody deserves to die that way. Regret what you did with her, but don't be ashamed of feeling her loss."

"You are a good woman, Sarah Fleischman."

"That's Cohen to you, young man."

A smile flickered across his face and, with his arms wrapped around Sarah's torso, Alex plotted how he would figure out who were the culprits and what he would do when he found them.

17

TO PUT THE events in Fort Lauderdale behind him, at least for a short while, Alex met Ezra and Massimo in Atlantic City. Before they arrived, he visited his own casino, The Shining Nugget, which was half a block away from the boardwalk in the heart of the East Coast gaming capital.

Alex checked out the first-floor reception and then headed past the premier restaurant and off to the gaming tables at the rear of the building. Everything was humming. All the tables were occupied and a glance at the cashiers showed him that the joint was generating gelt.

Safe knowing that the business was operating well front of house, Alex wandered back to reception and asked the woman at the main desk to let Lincoln Page know he had arrived. He sat in one of the plush armchairs and waited with a cigarette in his hand. Ten minutes later and Page surfaced from the bowels of the casino.

"We weren't expecting you so soon, Alex. I had been told you were coming tomorrow."

Alex shrugged.

"I was always due today. Your people had their wires crossed."

"Never mind, you are here and I am happy you are with us, of course."

"Is there a more private room than this lobby we could talk, Lincoln?"

The man nodded and took Alex behind the reception area and into the warren of corridors and rooms reserved for staff. They ended up in a poky space, which was big enough for a table and two chairs, but not much else.

"Is there anywhere less comfortable we could sit, Lincoln?"

The guy's expression showed he had no idea what point Alex was making and he let it go. There were more important matters to attend to.

Alex lit a cigarette and flicked the ash on the floor. Page sat in the other chair and waited, unconcerned by the mess piling up on the linoleum.

"How's business, Lincoln?"

"The take is on the up, so nothing to complain about. All is good, Alex."

"I figured, which is why I'm paying you a polite visit."

"Oh?"

"Yes, Lincoln. There is more money coming into this joint, but the appreciation you show me has not risen in the last three months. In fact, as we both know, your contribution has decreased over that period."

Alex waited because he had put enough men in the same situation to understand they needed a few minutes to ponder what he'd said to them and decide how they would respond. Page blinked twice and opened his mouth once, although no sound came out. He clamped his jaws tight again.

"Your silence is not helpful, Lincoln. All I ask is that you tell me why the skim has been light. Nothing more. Explain to me the situation and this conversation can be over."

Another blink.

"There have been some issues I needed to address."

"And they were more important than you meeting your obligations to me?"

Page's eyes headed to the floor and his cheeks glowed red.

"I had no choice, Alex."

"That may be so but the way I figure it, you owe me gelt for the last three months and your next payment is due at the end of the week too."

"Alex, I can't give you money I don't possess."

"That is a problem for you—but it is not my concern. On Friday, I expect to receive this month's payment and at least some of the restitution for your past failures."

"That's… I'm not sure whether I can do that, Alex."

"I am sure a man of your caliber will work something out. Banks offer great rates for loans nowadays, so I am told. I'll be back in two days to ensure that you pay what you owe."

Alex left The Shining Nugget knowing that there would be trouble with Page on Friday. He had arranged for Ezra and Massimo to be in town by then, anyway. Between the three of them, Alex was sure they could handle any fallout from Lincoln.

LINCOLN SAT IN a wooden chair facing Alex as Ezra and Massimo stood a few feet away. A cigarette hung from the corner of Page's mouth and they all heard him wheeze as he exhaled. The ash fell on his lap but he didn't pay no never mind to that as he had bigger concerns than a cleaning bill.

Massimo had tied the guy's hands behind his back and the man's ankles were strapped to the chair legs. Alex continued to stare at him but had not uttered a word since arriving in the wharf building some ten minutes before.

"I am glad we have this opportunity to discuss matters, Lincoln. When we spoke earlier in the week, you appeared reticent to make amends for the debt you had amassed over the previous three months. I am pleased that my colleagues grabbed your attention."

Page's eyes flitted right then left, as he checked out Massimo and Ezra, who remained still as rocks. With nothing remaining to smoke, Page spat the stub onto the floor. His breathing increased the instant the butt landed on the ground, and Alex speculated if the guy was about to have a heart attack. A minute later Page focused on Alex again.

"I told you it would be difficult for me to get any extra for you this week. If business was that good, then I wouldn't be in this room with you. We'd all be rolling in clover."

The casino manager had a point, but sometimes being right just isn't enough. Alex sighed.

"The problem I find with you, Lincoln, is not the lack of my money itself, although that is a situation with which we need to deal. My biggest issue is that you lied to me."

Alex raised a finger and Ezra launched himself at Page and slapped him hard on the right cheek with such force that the chair teetered and almost crashed to the floor.

"It is a question of trust."

Ezra used the back of his hand to hit Page's other cheek and, again, he came inches away from falling over, on the other side this time. The guy's breathing took a massive turn for the worse.

"You gotta believe me…"

"Lincoln, I accept you don't have my gelt. You are not so stupid that you would hold the money back to get this beating instead. And we've only just started."

Alex paused to give Ezra a moment to wallop Page's face a third time. An arc of red sprang from his cheek and landed on the wooden floor. A mouse observed the blood drip between the cracks in the floorboards. Massimo lit a cigarette.

"Now you are in this situation, you need to consider how you are going to get yourself out of it. We are talking about a question of trust, Lincoln."

He raised a finger and Ezra stepped back to resume his earlier position. Massimo inhaled deeply on his smoke. Silence filled the room as Alex watched Lincoln attempt to think.

FOUR HOURS LATER and Alex lit yet another cigarette. He looked at Page, only his head visible in the sand, and wondered if they should just kill him and be done with it.

"The tide will do the job for us, Alex. Besides, you said yourself this is a question of trust. If the guy had only withheld money from you, then yes, he could dig his own grave and we would shoot him in the head. But this was a different situation."

Alex nodded in agreement and threw his smoke into Lincoln's face. Sparks of hot tobacco flew into the air. That was not the first burn the guy had received that night, although he was unconscious at present and unable to experience the humiliation. They knew he'd wake up in time to drown.

In the car, Ezra drove them back to the center of Atlantic City and Alex offered them a bite to eat at his hotel. When they'd finished their dessert, he explained to them the real reason he had invited them over to the gaming capital of the East Coast.

"I wish to make good on my word and hand over the boardwalk casinos to your control. As we dealt with the last casino that was proving difficult, I can do this with a clean conscience."

"Thank you, Alex."

"*Gornisht*. It is nothing more than my attempt to keep my promise to you that you will inherit my illegal operations as I devolve my interests into more legitimate concerns."

18

WHEN ALEX ARRIVED in Miami, as ever, Tito met him at the airport and drove the saloon back home.

"All quiet while I've been away?"

"For sure. Moishe borrowed me for a brief trip—he was trying to impress his wife."

"The boy has no idea how to handle women."

Tito snorted and Alex tried to check his expression using the rear-view mirror, but no joy.

"I can tell you have spent some of the time taking a cloth to this jalopy."

"It's a beautiful vehicle and should be treated well."

"And how has Sarah been in my absence?"

"She has kept herself busy."

"Oh? Doing what?"

"This and that… I have been helping her learn Italian."

"She's expressed no interest in languages before."

"That woman has hidden depths."

Alex ground his molars at Tito's comment. Before he could respond, the automobile halted outside the house, and Tito scurried round to open the car door for his boss. Alex got out and popped inside, leaving the chauffeur to sort out his luggage.

HE FOUND SARAH on the patio with a mug of coffee in her hand. She smiled, stood up, and gave her returning warrior a big hug.

"Fancy a drink?"

Alex nodded and she called for the housekeeper.

"Veronica, will you make a fresh pot of coffee, please?"

"Would you like something to eat, too?"

"A cheese blintz and some orange juice. Plane food is filling but tasteless."

"How was your meeting with Ezra and Massimo?"

"After a minor local difficulty, I have now passed on my Atlantic City gaming interests to the pair of them. We are almost free and clear, Sarah."

"That leaves Vegas and not much else?"

"Yes, that's right. I'd like to keep it going until the New Year. Three more months of income will buy us a family vacation to look back on."

"Don't do it for me. I am happy if we spend a long weekend shopping in New York. I'm a girl of simple tastes."

Alex chuckled.

"You are many things, but you are not simple, Sarah. Besides, I gather Tito is teaching you Italian."

"Oh, I wouldn't quite put it that way. I was lying here yesterday afternoon when Tito walked through and we got talking. He shared a couple of phrases; nothing more than that."

He raised his eyebrows.

"He made it sound a lot more than that in the car… and what was he doing in this part of the grounds?"

"No idea, Alex. He came from the office building and headed off to the garage. I paid little attention to him."

"But he stayed a while? Sat down and chatted with you?"

"Five minutes, maybe. It's not like we spent the afternoon together, Alex."

"Sure, and he chauffeured Moishe and Alecia as well. Does he do that often, Sarah?"

"First that I've noticed. Is it important?"

"I don't know but he is getting mighty tight with my family when he is paid to look after my travel needs."

Sarah shrugged and took another sip of her coffee.

"HOW WAS THE flight back to Vegas, Massimo?"

"The usual, Alex. Are you calling about our Atlantic City business?"

"Not at all. I wanted to ask you about Tito. You knew him well before you let him go?"

"We weren't close, but we had worked together for a few years. Why?"

"I never found out why he needed to skip town in such a hurry. There were never any details."

A laugh on the other end of the line.

"Alex, I'm surprised you are asking me for references after all this time."

"It's nothing like that, old friend. I have no complaints about Tito's work, but I'd be interested to find out why he headed east."

"From what I recall, his girlfriend got pregnant and her dad was unimpressed with the way Tito handled the situation."

"How was that?"

"He told her to get an abortion and when she refused, Tito offered to push her down the stairs. I should add that the father came over from Sicily."

"Did she have the baby in the end? It'd be a couple of months old by now."

Silence on the line.

"I don't know. Not that I'm aware, but like I said, Alex, we were never that close. He was a good worker and knew how to drive. That's all I've got."

"Massimo, would you do me a favor and ask around if that kid turned up? I can't put my finger on it, but I have a feeling there's something not kosher about the man."

"Of course. If I pick up anything, I'll let you know."

"Go a step better than that, please. Find out by the weekend. I want this matter resolved."

ALEX RECEIVED A phone call on Sunday evening.

"Sorry it took me so long to get back to you, but I wanted to be certain of my facts."

"And what did you discover, Massimo?"

"Nothing."

"I don't understand."

"From what I can tell, he never even met Fiorella Vico."

"The girl?"

"Yep. And I made discreet inquiries with that walrus she has of a father."

"And bupkis?"

"Zip. Either the affair brought so much shame on the family that no one is prepared to acknowledge anything happened…"

"Or Tito lied."

"That's the shape of it, Alex. I apologize if he has placed you in a difficult situation. We took him at his word. It's not like he's the first fella to knock up a skirt and refuse to accept responsibility for the consequences of his actions."

"No apology required, Massimo. You must take a man at face value. Without that, he is nothing."

Alex returned to the house and settled in next to Sarah for an evening watching television. They sent Veronica home early because she might as well have a night off. Sarah volunteered to rustle something up if they were hungry afterward. Half an hour later, Tito popped his head around the door.

"Is there anything I can get you guys?"

"I didn't hear you come in."

"No, Alex, I used the patio entrance to the kitchen. Is that a problem?"

"Not at all, Tito. There's nothing we need you for tonight but fill the car with gas. Tomorrow we are going to Fort Lauderdale. There's a new deli that sells cheesecake to die for and I aim to get me a slice."

◆ ◆ ◆

THE NEXT MORNING, the two men left after Alex finished his breakfast and Tito drove them straight to Fort Lauderdale in under forty-five minutes, thanks to the I-95, which opened the previous year; Alex always preferred the scenic route.

Once in the city boundaries, he directed Tito to Pelham's on East Las Olas Boulevard between Third and Fourth Avenues. Tito parked by a fire hydrant outside the deli while Alex hopped out to grab himself some baked cheesecake.

Thirty minutes later, he had consumed a slice and considered it tasty enough to buy an entire round, which was contained in a white pastry box tied up with a pink ribbon.

"Worth the journey, boss?"

"Sure was. Before we go back home, there's some studio business I need to attend to."

Tito nodded and used his knowledge of the back streets to get them to their destination in under ten minutes, despite the Monday morning traffic. He parked in the lot and opened the door for Alex.

"You might as well come inside, Tito. I shall be at least an hour and there's no point you waiting in the car all that time. You can be warm instead."

"I don't want to get in anybody's way, Alex."

"That will not be a problem. In case you hadn't noticed, the lot is vacant because there are no productions taking place right now. The joint will be empty apart from the two of us."

Tito shrugged and reached into the front passenger seat for his newspaper.

"When you put it like that..."

ALEX BREEZED THROUGH the main reception and headed to his office, where he rifled through his bottom desk drawer until he found what he was looking for. Back to the main entrance of the building, but Tito was nowhere to be seen. Alex popped his head into two meeting areas but nothing. Then he stopped and asked himself where he would go if he was going to settle in for a long rest.

The actors' dressing rooms were close to the sets. The leads had their own private places and there were two sizable areas for the remainder of the cast. Alex headed for one door marked with a star on the front and, sure enough, Tito lay on a chaise longue holding his paper, staring at the racing results.

"Can I borrow you for a minute?"

"Sure thing."

The fella followed Alex over to the sets and they carried on walking until the two men were on the other side and out onto the back lot. Tito whistled under his breath.

"This is quite a place. I never knew how big it was."

"Tito, I am surprised you say that because I reckon you've been here before."

"Huh?"

"Remind me again why you had to leave Vegas in such a hurry."

"I was in a spot of bother with a girl."

"Are you talking about Fiorella Vico?"

"A fine piece of skirt."

"Tito, I wouldn't know because I've never met her. The problem is that neither have you."

Tito's cheeks whitened and his expression froze.

"Did you ever meet with Liddy?"

"Not at all, boss. The only times I caught sight of her was when she was in the back of the car with you."

"And you didn't supply her with smack?"

"You got this all wrong, Alex. I did nothing like that."

"Tito, the problem with being a liar is that once you are found out, there is nothing you can say that a man can trust anymore."

Tito opened his mouth to speak, then thought better of it.

"Who instructed you to kill Liddy?"

"I didn't murder her, Alex. Believe me."

Alex shook his head and whipped out the pistol he'd taken from his desk drawer. Tito grabbed for the inside of his jacket, but before he had the chance to pull out his piece, Alex shot him twice in the torso and he crumpled to the ground.

An hour later, Alex sat in the driver's seat of his car and headed home. There was no sign left that Tito had ever visited the film studio.

He buried the body in a quarry outside of town, and he knew how to clean up after himself and leave no trace of Tito's blood on the floor. Although he took the scenic route, Alex made good time and arrived home for a late lunch.

"Where's Tito?"

"We won't see him again, Sarah. He decided to stay in Fort Lauderdale."

19

"WHAT WAS IN Fort Lauderdale to make Tito want to move there?"

"Sarah, be careful of the questions that you ask."

She shrugged and continued to read her magazine. Alex sighed because he understood what the silence between them meant.

"There was an issue of trust if you must know."

"He has always been reliable around us."

"I agree he appeared most helpful, but some matters arose recently that threw his character into disrepute."

She put down her journal.

"The reason he left Vegas in a hurry? He said he was escaping his responsibilities as a man."

"He did, Sarah, but there was no woman. There was no pregnancy. He lied to Massimo."

"Alex, we all possess a dark past, and some of us try to hide it as much as possible." A brief smirk flew across her face but vanished when she saw Alex's stern expression.

"We still haven't found Liddy's killer and Tito had access."

"But no motive, Alex."

"That brings the conversation back to why the fella was so keen to head over to Florida."

"Did he confess?"

"Not in so many words."

"But you killed him anyway?"

"Someone sent him over to Miami to spy on our dealings, and possibly much worse. We could have kept him as bait to lure them out into the open, but Tito had inveigled his way into too many parts of our family. If he whacked Liddy, I couldn't afford for him to be so near to my children and our grandkids."

Sarah lit a cigarette and passed it to Alex. Then she got one for herself.

"You said that life was behind us, Alex."

"I want it to be, but sometimes you have to play the hand you're dealt."

"We live together, we love together, and we die alone."

"I need to mend some fences with Massimo. When we were catching Tito in his lie, I might have implied that the fella hadn't done a good job of vetting the guy."

THE FLIGHT TO Palm Springs was as quick as normal and the next day Alex arrived at his second home to wait for his lieutenants. They had arranged to meet at six, but two hours later and they were nowhere to be seen.

Alex popped out to buy a takeout pizza from a local restaurant and hoped that Massimo and Ezra would appear by the time he got to the house, but no joy. There was still no sign of them when he retired to bed.

As he had not planned on staying so long, Alex went to a diner for breakfast and returned to find another car parked in the drive.

"Thanks for dropping by, guys."

The two men made themselves comfortable by the pool. Massimo held a coffee mug and Ezra seemed to be nursing a beer. Alex wandered into the kitchen and grabbed the coffeepot Massimo had made for himself and poured a cup. Then he returned to the patio.

"Let us start proceedings by me apologizing to you, Massimo."

The Italian raised his eyebrows.

"I hope you didn't feel I was criticizing you when we were discussing Tito. My frustrations might have got the better of me."

"Thank you, Alex. There was a point when you seemed to want to make me responsible for not spotting Tito's lie."

Ezra slurped his beer loud enough to interrupt the conversation, and Alex stared at him.

"Did you get to the bottom of his story?"

"No, Ezra. But we don't need to worry about Tito anymore."

Ezra raised his bottle in the air in a mock toast, and the other two sipped their coffees. "*Lechayim,*" Alex muttered under his breath.

THEY POPPED OUT for lunch and hopped over to an Italian restaurant that served a decent steak and reasonable pasta. All three passed on dessert but said yes to coffee.

"We're glad you've come to visit us, Alex."

"Why's that, Ezra?"

"We appreciate gaining your Atlantic City activities and they will take a while to bed down, but I, for one, can't help remembering what you promised us all those years ago."

"That I would divest myself of all my illegal interests?"

"Yessir."

Alex stirred his coffee, even though it contained neither cream nor sugar.

"These things take time, Ezra. I constructed a tangled web and I must be careful how I unpick it."

"We have been waiting a while, Alex. And without complaint."

"I imagine you both wish to get your hands on the Vegas cash flow. That's the only major interest left from the old days. But these things can't be hurried."

"Cannot or will not?"

Daggers flew out of Alex's eyes to Ezra.

"To have value in the asset I give to you, you need to accept that there is more time to wait."

Massimo sipped his coffee.

"And is the only issue before us that we must be patient? Are there any matters of trust you need to air, Alex?"

"Fellas, my life and the lives of the members of my family have rested in your hands too many times over the years for you to need to ask me that question. Of course, I trust the two of you. How could I not?"

"Sometimes you make it hard for us to believe you, Alex."

He flicked between Ezra and Massimo to judge their mood by their faces. Neither looked him square in the eye.

"Until this moment, I never expected either of you would disbelieve me. You need to understand that when I say your day will come, then I mean it. Forget Tito. Forget Atlantic City. Alex Cohen is assuring you I shall hand over my Vegas interests to you when the time is right."

Massimo glanced at Ezra whose eyes remained fixed on his mug.

19

ALEX PUT HIS newspaper down and took a swig of coffee.

"Did you see this?"

He gestured at an article, but it was too far away for Sarah to read. He passed the paper over for her to get a good look.

"Why would the Feds bother to dredge up that old case?"

"Because they've wanted to take Meyer down for the last thirty years or more, and now they believe they've found their opportunity."

Alex grabbed a mouthful of bagel and leaned back in his chair, while she went through the news story again.

"The fella isn't in the country."

"I know, Sarah. He had the smarts to get out while the going was good. He always said the Feds would hunt him down one day."

"That man is a survivor. Is there even an extradition treaty between the US and Israel?"

"No idea, but I'll fly over and pay him a visit. Meyer needs his friends around him at times like this."

"Alex, what if they grab you too?"

"Before the authorities do that, they'd need to file charges. And as far as I know, I'm not even under investigation. Besides, they took their pound of my flesh a long time ago."

"What will we do if they decide to re-open the old files they have on you?"

"Sarah, let's not get ahead of ourselves. I'm divested from almost all my illegitimate activities, and there is a web of companies, many offshore, between those revenue streams and anything with my name on it."

"If you go, I'm scared I'll never see you again."

"Don't worry, Sarah. Consider it as a vacation before Thanksgiving."

"So I'm coming too?"

"If it makes you happy, of course."

THE COUPLE LANDED in Tel Aviv and headed over to Herzliya, where Meyer had ensconced himself and his wife, Thelma in a villa.

"The place is big enough for an army, Alex. You and Sarah are welcome to stay here while you are on vacation. It's so large, we'd spend days under the same roof and not bump into each other."

"We don't want to be any trouble, Meyer."

"Sarah, that is kind of you to say, but we all know that hosting the pair of you is nothing compared to the difficulties that are storing up for me back in the States."

"Isn't this your home under the Right to Return law?"

"Thelma and I filled out the forms, but Golda has yet to place the appropriate stamps on the pieces of paper."

"You know her?"

"Now why would you be surprised at that fact, Sarah?"

"You've only been here a few months and already you are on first-name terms with the prime minister."

"She and I go way back. It's nothing, but she is holding out on me and I don't understand the reason."

AFTER DINNER, THELMA and Sarah moved to a balcony and left the fellas on their own. Meyer held a cigar and Alex sipped his Scotch on the rocks.

"Who'd have imagined the Feds would need to go back to the Flamingo to get you on the hook, Meyer?"

"That place is jinxed. First there was Benny and now me."

"To be fair, Meyer, we both know what did for our dear partner and it wasn't malicious spirits in the casino he built."

Meyer lowered his eyes as he recalled his friend and the Havana conference where his fate was sealed by Charlie Lucky and the rest of what was then called the syndicate.

"The irony is that I offered to give you all the tax receipts you needed back when we still had Prohibition. I figured I had every angle covered."

"Meyer, how could you guess that decades later, some rat would drop a dime to save his own skin? Do you know who did the deed?"

"Vinnie Teresa."

"Never heard of him."

"A nobody loan shark until he testified against me. Now he's a hero of law enforcement."

"Is it his word against yours or is there other evidence?"

"My lawyer tells me that his testimony is sufficient to sink my ship."

"If only Mendy Greenberg was still alive."

"God rest his soul, Alex. But he couldn't keep you out of stir."

"No, but he told me years later how you softened my landing in Sing Sing."

Meyer shrugged to dismiss the comment as though it were nothing.

"Would you like me to have a word with Vinnie?"

"Alex, what is important to me is that you don't get involved. The last thing we need is for you to be caught up in this mess. Besides, it's not a conversation with you that I fear."

Both men smiled at each other, aware not just of what Alex was capable but secure knowing that there were many hits to his name. From Alex's perspective, the least he could do was to whack the scum that threatened his friend.

THE FOLLOWING DAY, Alex and Sarah walked along the Herzliya beach, enjoying the evening air. They had spent their time with Meyer, who took them around Tel Aviv like tourists.

"What do you expect he'll do, Alex?"

"Fight tooth and nail to stay in this country. I can't imagine he will want to take on a tax evasion court case. They have a witness who'll say that Meyer handled the Flamingo skim."

"It's crazy that they haven't indicted him for stealing from the casino; only for not declaring the tax he should have paid on the earnings."

"We live in a remarkable world, Sarah."

"Will he be safe here?"

"You would assume that he has donated enough money to the state of Israel over the decades that the least they can do is grant him the citizenship that every Jew is given. It is what Golda Meir fought for not so long ago and why this country exists."

"Alex, that was over thirty years in the past. I hope I'm wrong, but I imagine that the current government feels less indebted to Meyer than he might assume."

"My money's on Meyer. Always has been and always will."

November 1971

20

AS THE HOST, Alex had the honor of slicing the turkey as the extended household celebrated Thanksgiving. Moishe, Alecia, and Oscar were present, along with David, Dorit, and their kids Jojo and Nathan. A family gathering couldn't rightly happen without Alex's sister, Esther, in tow.

"To happiness and freedom."

His toast was echoed by everybody in the room and everyone tucked into the feast Veronica had prepared for them. The grandkids were old enough to understand they needed to remain seated for the entire meal and not run around like possessed demons.

As dessert was served, Alex sat back and surveyed the scene with his extended family chatting away and at peace with each other. Of course, his estranged siblings were nowhere to be found, but they had only seen each other on one occasion as adults. That was normal for Alex, although he knew Sarah wished he had used his mother's funeral as a catalyst to reconnect with Aaron and Reuben.

Everyone sat at the long rectangular table which filled the large dining room and Sarah had planned the seating so that couples were opposite each other, with Esther and the kids in between, and Sarah and Alex at each of the shorter ends. He watched as Moishe winked at Alecia after he made a saucy comment to Nathan that went over the boy's head. Alex smiled.

They formed a good couple, even though they only had one child. His son had come a long way from being a pain-in-the-ass firebrand when he was a teenager. Same with David, but he had always known he would make something of himself.

WITH THE MEAL over, the women and children retired to the patio and left Alex and his sons to smoke cigars at the table.

"Are these Cuban?"

"That joke never gets old, does it, Moishe?"

He chuckled to himself and nodded.

"Enough time has passed for you to find the funny side, Pop."

"As someone who didn't flee for his life, I imagine that's exactly what you would expect."

Moishe's cheeks reddened, and he took another sip from his Scotch.

"Don't worry, Moishe. I'm messing with you. It's a great joke, if only you'd checked the label, you would have seen you are right. They are from Cuba."

Now it was David's turn to laugh. "He got you."

"Nicely played, Pop."

A few minutes later and the three men sank into their drinks and conversation halted. Alex punctured the silence and raised the mood.

"Mighty fine smoke."

They all chuckled again and Moishe's eyes lit up, sparkling at his father.

"How are we getting on making you legal, Pop?"

"David, I'm just left with my Las Vegas interests. There's nothing else to sort out."

"Pop, why are you still connected to all those gambling operations? I've warned you repeatedly about the RICO laws that are in place."

"David, it's never that easy. If I only owned the casinos, then all I would need to do would be to find a buyer who was eligible to hold a gaming license."

"I know, Pop."

"But there is no piece of paper in existence that shows what I do. Instead, the details of my involvement are embedded in the mind of every mob boss on the East and West Coasts."

"So tell them you are quitting and someone else must take over."

"Moishe, the Vegas skim is a house of cards. Any slight movement and the whole matter comes crashing down at our feet. My intention is to insert Ezra and Massimo in my place, but the time has to be right. The bosses are used to dealing with them, but the thing that keeps Vegas running so smoothly is that my word and my oversight are backing any significant piece of action in Nevada."

"What do you mean? I understood you just were skimming the take?"

"Moishe, I do not want to go into too many details, because then you will know too much about my less licit affairs…"

"What Pop is trying to say is that Vegas is an open city. It is not owned by any one mob. They all play well together only while someone stands in the middle of any transactions between them. And that person keeps the peace if there are any disagreements. That, Pop does."

Alex nodded and sipped his Scotch.

"And I would guess until the mob bosses view Ezra and Massimo with the same respect they show Pop, then he can't step away."

"Listen to your brother. The time he spent in Havana with me opened his eyes to a world I never wanted either of you to witness or be a part of. That is my shame."

ONCE EVERYBODY HAD gone home, Alex and Sarah helped Veronica clear up. A glance at the clock told them what they already knew—it was very late and time to go to bed.

When Alex got under the covers, Sarah was asleep. Or so he believed. She turned round to face him.

"I overheard David and Moishe talking tonight. They said you are holding back from divesting your Vegas operation because of your concern over leaving a power vacuum."

"You might well have heard correctly. That is what I told them, although not in so many words."

"Alex, is it not true then?"

He sighed because it was past midnight and he was too tired for this kind of conversation.

"There is an element of truth in what I said. But the main reason I have done nothing about Vegas is because I keep getting sidetracked by other matters. Extricating myself from Vegas is difficult and requires all my concentration to enable the status quo to be maintained once I've left."

"What else is there, Alex?"

"This thing with Meyer, for one. The Feds are prepared to go back to ancient history to indict members of the old guard. They might already have caught me for tax evasion, but what else have they got up their sleeves? On top of that, there are new laws the federal government has put in place just to catch mobsters. And they can dig into your past for decades in order to dredge up some felony that slipped through their fingers."

Sarah rested her hand on his arm.

"If that was not enough to keep me awake at night, the authorities have got members of the mob to rat out their old pals. That's why Meyer is in schtuck."

"You told me you'd always been careful."

"Of course I have, but that doesn't mean some lowlife desperate to cut a deal can't remember seeing something I've done which isn't on the up and up. All it takes is for one fella to turn on his compatriots and we are all sunk."

"But, Alex, if you separate yourself from Vegas, won't that make it harder for the Feds to connect you with anything from your past?"

"If I do untangle myself from Nevada, then I will only taste the sensation of freedom. I shall remain shackled because I need to ensure that between RICO laws and rats, they can't get me. You and the rest of the family won't be safe from their grasp until there is a sufficient gulf between me and all the nefarious activities of my past."

Sarah held him in her arms for a long while.

"How much time do you believe it will take?"

"I wish I knew. This is the second time in a month I wished Mendy Greenberg was still alive because his devious legal mind is what I need right now. My biggest problem at this point is Tito."

"Why mention him?"

"I don't know who he worked for or what he was doing around us. He refused to confess to Liddy's murder, even though he must have known he was going to die. I can't help wondering if he was planted by the Feds, or by an Italian mob."

"What would the mafia gain by doing that?"

"Intelligence about Vegas, I guess. I don't have this all figured out, but I am surprised the cops haven't come gunning for me. They must know most of what I've done and Bobby Kennedy may be dead, but the FBI sure is concerned with bringing the mobs down to size. I'm the perfect target."

"We should move to Israel and be rid of all this *tsoris*.

"Meyer has shown us that running away doesn't stop the aggravation. All that happens is you end up paying more pinheads to bail you out."

"David is guaranteed a job for life."

"Moishe too. Even if they squander all the family's gelt, the world always needs lawyers and accountants. Sarah, there is too much of you inside them for this to be a worry. David believes he is borrowing the money from his children and grandchildren yet to be born. Moishe is a Jewish accountant. What else can he be but tight with gelt?"

SEPTEMBER 1972

21

ALEX RECEIVED TWO phone calls one day after the other. The first brought him good news from Israel. Lansky had got through his open heart surgery.

"He might be small, but that man is a bull, Sarah."

"Ever since I've known him, Meyer has always been a fighter."

This put a smile on Alex's face, which hadn't been seen for several months. He continued to juggle the complexities of removing himself from the Vegas operation.

The next day's call wiped the grin off his expression.

"Alex, this is Eugenio Martinez."

He blinked for a second, not recognizing the name, then it all came back to him. Alex recalled leaping out of the boat onto the beach in the Bay of Pigs. He led his men over the south of the island for as long as possible before they were forced to pull out. Martinez was one of the few in his group to survive that night.

"Pleased to hear from you after so many years. How did you get this number?"

"A mutual friend suggested I speak with you."

"What about?"

"You won't find this in the papers yet, but some of us from the old days were arrested for burglarizing the Democratic National Committee's headquarters in Washington."

"The what?"

A sigh.

"The Democratic Party's offices. I thought you would continue to follow politics, even now."

"My interest in those matters died the day we hauled ourselves off that beach."

"Understood, Alex, but you still support old friends?"

"I do my best, but make no promises. Tell me what the situation is and I'll see what I can do."

"Our mutual friend told me you had connections in high places who could help me wriggle off this hook."

"Where are you, Eugenio?"

"Washington, of course. I'm out on bail. The grand jury meets in a few days and I need your influence to get out of this thing. I don't want to go to jail."

"Nobody ever does, Eugenio. I'll fly up today and we can talk some more without a phone line getting in the way."

MARTINEZ APPEARED HAGGARD when Alex walked up to him at a pre-arranged diner on the outskirts of the city center. They ordered a coffee each and waited for the waitress to leave them alone before starting any conversation.

"This is a public place you've chosen, Eugenio. And right at the front."

"Alex, a table is a table. Don't concern yourself with trivia so."

He raised an eyebrow at the Cuban and sipped his coffee. It was burned, but he chose not to call the waitress back to complain. The drink was not the purpose of his visit.

"Now I am here, out in the open. I assume we can talk more freely than on the phone."

"More or less, Alex."

"Do you think you've been followed?"

Alex glanced around in case he spotted Eugenio's tail.

"I haven't felt alone since the night we were arrested."

"Although I have no desire to learn the details and get indicted myself, tell me what happened."

Martinez sighed and took a gulp of his coffee.

"There isn't much to say. We went into the building, did what we had to do, and were about to leave when a night watchman found us and all hell broke loose."

"Did they find any loot on you?"

"None"

"But you had your tools with you."

"Yes. Only…"

Alex raised a hand to halt Eugenio in his tracks.

"If you aren't going to give me everything on a silver platter, then let me figure it out for myself."

Martinez closed his mouth and allowed Alex to continue.

"Have you confessed to anything and are they putting you under any pressure to rat out the others?"

"No and no. That isn't my problem, Alex."

"What is? If you keep your piehole shut, the most they might get you on is attempting to burglarize an office. Was there cash to steal?"

"I wouldn't know. We didn't look."

Now it was Alex's turn to be silent.

"Eugenio, what spooked you so much that you called a mutual acquaintance to put you in touch with me?"

"Let's say that I've seen Gerry Droller twice since we came back from the Bay of Pigs and both times were in the last seven days."

Now Alex did more than glance around the diner. The man was the lynchpin of the CIA effort to oust Castro from Cuba, and that entire operation was his baby. Alex assumed he had seen the back of that guy. Matters had got very serious, very quickly.

"Who is our mutual friend?"

"Sam. He told me you were in with Droller, so I figured you could find out whether the man is on my side."

"Giancana thinks too much of me, Eugenio. You've seen Gerry more times than me since we left the carnage on that island."

Martinez sighed and cast his eyes down into his lap. Alex's mind swarmed with potential worries.

"You said you noticed him twice. What happened?"

"This is tricky, Alex, because you don't want to know what I was doing in the Watergate building."

"He sent you there?"

Martinez nodded, just the once.

"Are you with the firm?"

"Don't make me answer that question, Alex. It's all too complicated."

"When did you see Droller last?"

"In the police station. When the local cops interrogated me, they left the interview room door open a while. He was in the corridor talking to the lieutenant, who later asked me a bunch of questions and then they let me go."

"How long did it take before you were released?"

"An hour, maybe two."

"That wasn't much time for what comes across as a small-time crime. Wouldn't you expect to be thrown into a holding cell for the rest of the day until they got round to your paperwork?"

"I suppose."

"So, Eugenio, who greased the machine to make it operate that fast?"

Martinez's eyes darted left, then right.

"I have no idea. I was so pleased to be free that I didn't consider that part."

"It must have been a friend in law enforcement."

"If I had such a buddy, we wouldn't be sitting here in the first place, Alex."

The waitress arrived to offer a top-up of their mugs, but Alex declined.

"Only the check when you are ready, thanks."

Martinez looked askance at Alex.

"Aren't you going to help me?"

"Eugenio, I have no connections with the CIA and so there is nothing I can do for you. Droller is part of my past. Even if I wanted to, I've no clue how to get in contact with the guy—apart from asking that lieutenant if he has Gerry's number."

"Would you do that for me?"

Alex shook his head.

"I'm no longer in that business so my hands are tied. I wish you well and hope the grand jury doesn't find sufficient evidence that much of a crime was committed. It sounds to me they've only got you for attempted burglary, but I'm no lawyer."

He threw some bills down on the table to cover the coffees and a healthy tip, and Alex left the diner.

ALEX WALKED AWAY and headed two blocks east, one south and three east again. Only after this zigzag journey did he stop to hail a cab to take him back to the airport.

Then there was the interminable wait in line at the sales desk and Alex did his best to remain patient, despite his belief that every second spent in Washington brought him a step nearer to his past. Thinking about it, he had been wrong about Droller.

There was a moment in the corridor on Bobby Kennedy's last night on this earth that Alex saw the guy. He never figured out what the CIA was doing in the Ambassador Hotel in Los Angeles and he brushed past the agent as he escaped from the assassination.

As he scanned the terminal building, Alex thought he saw a face he recognized in the crowd. Was that Droller? He closed his eyes and opened them a second later. The guy had vanished or was never there in the first place, but Alex took no chances. He stepped out of the line and headed for the taxi rank. With eyes plastered at the back of his head, Alex only waited two minutes before he was in a cab.

"Where do you want to go, Mac?"

"You know any car rentals in town?"

"Reckon I might, bud."

"Then let's stop talking and you start driving."

When they arrived, Alex paid the guy to wait five minutes. Nobody seemed to have followed them, but he took no chances and got the driver to take him to a second rental location before giving him a handsome tip.

"Here's my card, Mac. Any time you're in town, you call me and I'll chauffeur you all day."

"I don't plan to return to this city as long as I live, but thanks anyway."

December 1973

22

ALEX AND SARAH divided their time between the US and Israel. With the events in the film studio receding from his memory, he sold up his interests and concentrated on his family and friends, although he maintained a careful eye on Vegas.

"Meyer, thanks for finding this place for us."

"Gornisht. What are buddies for, right?"

"We expected we'd get tied up in Israeli red tape."

"I might not be able to obtain residency for myself, Alex, but I still have the ability to grease the wheels of bureaucracy."

"Much appreciated. And we are a short walk from your home too."

"I would be foolish to find you a place far away from me."

Meyer smiled at his old friend.

"Tell me if you require any help to furnish the joint. There are some people in Herzliya I can recommend."

"I figured you might."

"Sarah, there is no need to take that tone with me."

They chuckled for a moment because all three had known each other for decades and were at ease in each other's company, despite what they had been through in Cuba.

"I'm leaving all that sort of thing to Sarah. I've forgotten the last time my opinion was sought."

"Alex, would you like to talk to me about colors and cushions?"

"Now I remember why you don't ask me; I plain don't care."

LESS THAN A month after signing the deeds, Alex and Sarah moved into their new home and invited Meyer and Thelma over for a meal to celebrate. As well as fixing all the interior, Sarah had also flown Veronica over as there wasn't much for her to do in their Miami home, and everything to do in Herzliya.

"Thank you for a lovely dinner, Sarah."

"You're welcome, Meyer. I don't believe I've ever been able to host a get-together with the four of us."

"When I lived in Florida, I was always concerned about prying eyes. There are no such worries over here."

"The Feds?"

"Yes, Alex. And I wasn't wrong, was I?"

"For all those years, you came across as paranoid."

"But it was Vinnie's testimony rather than surveillance footage that the FBI is using to get to you, right?"

"Yes, Sarah."

Alex was the first to laugh and Meyer held out as long as possible but got the joke in the end.

"All those years spent inside that house and I should have been on a golf course or in a casino. You know what you should have done for me, Alex?"

"What?"

"You should have killed that scumbag Vinnie."

Alex stopped laughing. "Give me the word and I will still do that for you."

Meyer smiled and pointed at him. "Gotcha."

They all chuckled some more until the laughs died down and Veronica cleared the dessert plates away. Then the men went for a stroll around the neighborhood, while Sarah and Thelma sat outside and chatted over another bottle of red wine.

TWO WEEKS LATER, Ezra and Massimo paid Alex a visit, and he offered to put them up in the new place, but they preferred a nearby hotel.

"How are you pair doing?"

"Just fine, thank you, Alex. I notice there are some candles lit."

"For Hanukkah. It's not my thing, but it's impossible to avoid in Israel. Christmas doesn't do it for me in the US either."

"I feared you might have found God."

Alex laughed at Ezra's comment.

"Not that I've noticed."

"This is a fine house, Alex. Congratulations to you and Sarah."

"Thank you, Massimo. Given the problems back home, I figured it can't be a bad idea to own a bolthole far from American law enforcement."

"That makes sense for those who can afford it."

"Ezra, I am sure you have a tidy nest egg hidden away somewhere in an offshore account. I reckon you could buy yourself a second home. Or should I say, third house because you also own real estate for your mistress? I'm just saying; we are all friends here."

His old lieutenant was silent for a spell, and Alex couldn't tell if he was sulking like a tyke. Massimo picked up where Alex's acid comment had left off.

"Alex, none of us is suffering from a lack of cash, but some have more control over our lives than others."

"Is that some kind of jibe at me?"

"Take it however you want but we've been waiting for more years than either of us remember for you to hand over the reins in Vegas. Every month we deliver the goods for you, but our Italian business partners perceive your ongoing involvement as weakness on our part."

"Massimo, I appreciate that this matter has caused both of you significant inconvenience, but you have shown understanding and patience with my situation."

"Until now. We can't wait forever, Alex."

"Ezra, if I didn't know you better, I'd feel you were threatening me."

Massimo lit a cigarette and refused to make eye contact, while Ezra stared at Alex without blinking.

"It is not a threat. As you said, we are all friends here, but we are expressing our concern. If the situation doesn't change soon, then we won't have much motivation to keep the operation running smoothly. We all know that we have all made enough gelt to not need any more."

"Massimo, you fellas would be prepared to run the business into the ground rather than wait a little longer?"

"Five years, Alex. That's the time we've been tapping our toes. And we aren't suggesting we'd destroy the enterprise, but you forget the effort it takes each day to protect your interests from the Italian mobs, no offense, Massimo."

"None ever taken, Ezra."

"Look, Alex. All we are reminding you is that we need you to keep your word and pass over the operation to us. Every day you don't, we get weakened and we all know what happens when the mob smells weakness."

Massimo passed his hand in front of his throat, and Alex swallowed hard.

23

THE DISQUIET CREATED by his lieutenants' visit remained although Alex didn't want to believe that they might take any action. He and Sarah carried on regardless and plowed the small furrow of their lives in Herzliya.

He visited Meyer almost every day over the following weeks. In the pit of his stomach, he figured it best to stay close to his friend.

"I have an investment opportunity for you, Alex."

"Oh? I only buy into legal properties nowadays, you remember?"

"And that is why I am telling you about it. As someone applying for residency, I don't want to appear to offer a large sum of money to anyone in power in this country. Not yet, at any rate."

"What's the story?"

"This one is very simple. There is a diamond operation, which is poised to go great guns with a little seed investment."

"Tell me more, Meyer."

"They import gems from around the world, process them, and supply them to local jewelers."

"If it is all going so well, why do they need more cash?"

"An injection of capital would enable them to ramp up production and give them the chance to distribute cut diamonds across the globe."

"Arrange a visit and I'll take a look and tell you what I think. How much gelt are they seeking?"

"A million dollars."

ALEX AND SARAH borrowed Meyer's driver, Noori, to take them to Tel Aviv, where the headquarters of Shalev Laboratories were located. The owner, Yaffe Shalev, met them at the building's reception and took them through to the labs where the diamonds were brought in and cleaned before being cut.

Alex feigned interest, but he was less concerned about the exact details of what happened in the building than he was to judge the man who put his family name on the nameplate outside it. In contrast, Sarah was fascinated to watch how those white crystals turned into something pretty to rest on her finger or dangle from her ears.

Yaffe spoke excellent English and Alex understood why Meyer had insisted there would be no need for a translator to come along too.

"And now we can go to the next room where there is extra security, so forgive my people while they vacuum your clothing."

"You're kidding, Yaffe?" But he was not and everyone, including the owner, was subjected to intensive cleaning. Ten minutes of sucking later and they reached the other side of the process.

"Each day we recover up to five hundred dollars of diamond powder."

"Right, but it's not like you can glue the grains together and make a fresh necklace out of it."

"No, but diamonds remain super hard, even when they are tiny. The dust is used on grinding wheels and for polishing."

"Nice touch, Yaffe."

"It is the details you have to take care of, Alex."

The second room comprised several rows of benches, where a string of men were huddled over lintless cloths and sparkling gems.

"These are the best jewelers I can find in the diamond capital of the Middle East. Some have relocated from Amsterdam and New

York. Their task is simple: convert the gems they receive into the largest, most expensive, highest-rated diamonds that are possible."

"How can you trust they won't palm one? There are hundreds of stones in this place."

Yaffe nodded and pointed at the corners of the room, where several men dressed in black slacks and white linen shirts stood around.

"Each member of the security detail is tasked with watching a specific area of this place."

"And who watches the watchers?"

Shalev's eyes lifted to the ceiling and Alex noticed the cameras discreetly deployed. *This setup is just like a casino.*

"I can understand why Meyer recommended we should get together."

"I wish to expand and you want to invest, Alex. What's not to like?"

He raised a finger in the air at Yaffe.

"I'm considering an investment. Nothing has been agreed and I may do nothing."

"Of course, but I assume we are talking because you remain interested in my enterprise. If not, and I say this with all the respect that a friend of Meyer's deserves, you might as well leave now and I'll do something more useful."

"Is there somewhere to eat in this place?"

NOORI DROVE THE three of them to Dizengoff Street, just north of the square. "This is like a Jewish Fifth Avenue."

Sarah was right. They may not have been able to understand the Hebrew signs, but both Alex and Sarah recognized expensive clothes and upmarket cafes when they drove past them.

Yaffe indicated to Noori that he should pull over on the corner of Ben Gurion Boulevard and Dizengoff, leafy but dripping in gelt. Into a restaurant and over to the milk side, because Alex knew he'd want cheesecake for dessert. The couple had lived in Israel long enough to know that kosher food establishments split into meat and milk halves, as only in the latter were patrons allowed to eat dairy.

Although he fancied a steak, they were in a city port and he knew the quality of the fish would be exceptional; Sarah often chose salmon anyway. After the waitress took their order, the two men felt comfortable talking.

"How did you get started, Yaffe?"

"I learned all I know about diamonds from my father in a jeweler's he owned a few blocks from here."

Sarah's eyes glanced toward Yaffe's hand gesture, but Alex remained transfixed on his face.

"When he died, I took over the store…"

"And focused on the wholesale side of the business."

"My old man spent his entire life bent double over a bench in the rear of that place and I had no desire to repeat that mistake."

"Mine was a tailor who couldn't get work after we fled the pogroms and arrived in New York."

"Times were tough back then, I guess."

"Because of my position in the local community, Yaffe, I could help him find employment."

"Mazel tov on your good fortune."

"We have all worked hard to get to where we are. I am interested in considering where you and I might go together."

The waitress returned to deliver their main courses and then vanished as soon as she was able. Sarah chowed down while the other two continued their discussion.

"Yaffe, you have conquered Israel and now you want to take on the world. Is that fair?"

"More or less, Alex, although I wouldn't pretend to have cornered the market here. Not by a long step, but there's an enormous world out there and I reckon it'll be easier to be a small fish in a large pond than the other way around. Have you noticed how many gem merchants we have in this city?"

Alex shook his head but knew Tel Aviv was a major diamond center and had studied with his own eyes the current scale of Yaffe's operation. The guy had talent and ambition.

"Before the cheesecake arrives, let me ask one last question, Yaffe."

The Israeli raised his eyebrows with expectation.

"Are you speaking with any other potential backers?"

"Not at present, Alex."

"If you are, then that is fine, but I won't get involved in any bidding war. I am happy to pursue a positive resolution to this with you, but if you don't want us to work together, then just say so and I will walk away with no hard feelings and a full stomach."

OUTSIDE THE RESTAURANT, everybody shook hands. Yaffe refused Alex's offer to drop him back at his lab as he preferred to hike over to his father's store. It was still held in the family but run by his brother. A useful consumer outlet for anything that Yaffe wanted to keep from wholesale fingers.

"These sidewalks are as wide as in midtown Fifth Avenue."

"Yeah, this place is like a foreign New York, Sarah."

Alex lit cigarettes for them both as they stood while Yaffe sauntered down the road.

"The pace of life is a little slower than in the Big Apple though."

Sarah nodded in agreement. When they'd finished their smokes, the couple walked hand-in-hand to Noori's car, which was parked ten feet down the street. Their chauffeur spotted their impending arrival and scooted out of the vehicle and ran round to open the passenger door for them.

Alex patted Sarah's back to indicate she should get in first and, as she bent down, there was a flash as something sped by his head. The bang erupted half a breath later, and he pushed Sarah downward. Then he threw himself on top of her.

Another zing and a second bullet flew past them. Passersby scattered and high-net-worth shoppers screamed. Some slammed to the ground and others tried to run away.

"Where's the shooter?"

"Beats me, Alex."

"I reckon the slugs came from the other side of the street, Noori."

The chauffeur had drawn his weapon, but there was no sign of an assailant. Alex looked down and discovered a ripple of blood on Sarah's forehead.

"Are you—"

"Don't worry. I banged my head on the car on the way down. It's only a scratch."

He held her in his arms and hugged his wife like there was no tomorrow.

"I thought I might have lost you."

"This is the second time that someone has fired at you and almost caught me. You'd better not make this a habit."

He recalled the attack before the divorce that almost sealed the end of their relationship. And then the image of Rebecca bleeding in his arms a decade or two later. A tear fell from Alex's eye and dropped to the ground.

24

HAVING RECOVERED FROM the shock and returned to Herzliya, Alex set to work figuring out what had happened. First item on the agenda was to find a doctor to check out Sarah and Alex was relieved that her initial assessment was supported by medical expertise.

"Meyer, who would have done this?"

"I've spoken with Noori, who has some contacts with the military, if you get my meaning."

"Mossad?"

Meyer's eyes refused to meet Alex's gaze, which spoke volumes.

"He is making inquiries on our behalf. If anyone can find out anything, then he is the man."

"I didn't think I had been here long enough to make any enemies, Meyer."

"In that case, the source of the problem is back in the States, especially if you have been focusing your energy on legitimate activities."

"Do you reckon the mob has put out a contract on me?"

"After all these years, who knows what those Italians think? But in the old days, a member of Murder Corporation would have at least left you critically wounded."

Alex nodded, but couldn't help feeling Meyer was too quick to discount the commission. Since Sam Giancana's warning to stay away from the mafia bosses, Alex had expended much effort following that advice, as he had no intention of being buried in a desert someplace or having his skeleton discovered in the Everglades in a decade or two. But he had dabbled in adult entertainment.

"What if it were Ezra or Massimo?"

"Has it come to this, Alex?"

"I don't need to be a trained psychologist to know they were mighty angry with me when we met last. Both lieutenants want me to relinquish control of Vegas. Perhaps they tired of waiting."

"I assumed they were always loyal to you."

"They have been, Meyer, until now."

"I SHOULDN'T BE bedridden, Alex. The doctor was clear I can be up and about."

"One day's rest is not too much to ask, Sarah. There is no need for you to get fatigued. Besides, you are calm about being shot at. The last time this happened, we ended up divorced."

She smiled and nodded.

"A lot of water has passed under several bridges since that night, Alex. Times have changed and I trust you more."

"Thank you for that."

"No one is perfect, and we all make mistakes, but you have spent too many years trying to go straight for me to believe it is all a sham. Your heart is in the right place."

"So you'll stay in bed today?"

"I'll finish this lunch and then I'm getting up. I will climb the wall if I remain in this room a minute after that."

As much as Alex wished to coddle Sarah in cotton wool, he knew his wife better than to stop her from doing what she wanted. He bit his tongue and helped her get ready before they sat outside for a while and then Sarah demanded they go for a stroll.

"Now, this is where I must insist that we remain inside the grounds of the villa, Sarah."

"You aren't being fair. We both know I am more than well enough to take a walk around the block."

"It's not about your health, Sarah. This is about who shot at us yesterday. Until we find out their identity, we need to play things safe. And now is not the time for idle promenades."

She was silent for a spell, and then she shrugged.

"A walk around the garden then?"

"I knew you'd see it my way in the end."

THE SCRATCH ON Sarah's head faded within a week and soon after, Noori paid Alex a visit to give him an update on what his secret service colleagues had found out.

"First, Alex, we know for definite that this was no Israeli killer."

"How are you so certain?"

"The fact you are alive is evidence enough, but witnesses observed a man in his twenties running from the scene with a black violin case."

"I've done it myself, back in the day, Noori."

"He was European or American, not Middle Eastern."

"And not Arab looking?"

"Not at all. Were you expecting an Arabic hit?"

"No, but I have a long list of people who would want to have me buried in the ground."

Noori grunted and carried on with his report.

"Further investigation showed the guy had flown in from Chicago a week ago. Although we can't be certain, it is a fair guess that he has been biding his time since then for the hit."

"He wasn't a lone gunman out for revenge because of some slight by me to his mother or sister, or some other family member?"

"Of that, I am less sure. The good news is that we can find out without breaking a sweat, Alex."

"How so?"

"He made the mistake of going to an airport under the same name he flew into the country. We are holding him in Jerusalem."

"We?"

"Two trusted individuals. The less you know, the better for all concerned, but I vouch for them."

◆ ◆ ◆

THREE HOURS LATER and Noori drove Alex to the Jewish quarter in the Israeli capital. Down a rabbit warren of streets until he parked, and they took the last five minutes by foot. A nondescript house that looked like any other in the area was their destination. Noori had his own keys, and they went straight to the basement.

A single bare lightbulb hanging from the ceiling provided Alex with all the illumination he needed. They joined three guys, all sitting, but as they arrived, two stood up and the third remained unconscious.

"Is he…?"

"Only resting, Alex. He has received a severe beating, which is how we know what we do about him, but these men are professionals. They don't kill informants without permission. Can I get you a coffee while we give him a chance to rest?"

Fifteen minutes later and Noori served drinks for everyone, apart from the stranger. A few sharp slaps around the face and the man awoke from his slumber. Although Noori offered him a chair, Alex remained standing.

"What is your name?"

"Ponzio Arnoni."

"Do you know who I am?"

"Alex Cohen."

"The man you tried to kill."

Arnoni opened his mouth and closed it again.

"Who sent you, Ponzio?"

"Nobody."

"Ponzio, the more you lie, the greater the pain you will experience. I shall ask you again. Who put the contract out on me?"

"No one, and that's the truth."

"You expect me to believe that you came over to this country to assassinate me all by yourself? With no help and no reason?"

"There was no hit, but I had a reason."

"Ponzio, you need to explain yourself before I grow impatient."

To emphasize Arnoni's predicament, Alex nodded at Noori, who issued an instruction in Hebrew to the other two. One of them lit a cigarette and stubbed it out on Ponzio's palm, who let out a scream that sent a chill down Alex's spine. He had forgotten the sound of torture.

"I heard some important people talking about you, Alex. How their lives would be better if you were dead. So I thought I would get into their good books and sort the matter out."

"What were these men saying about me?"

"The older man said he was spending a lot of capital on preventing the commission from whacking you. The second fella offered to kill you, and the old one told him not to bother."

"But you were prepared to go to the trouble for the sake of upping your status in the mob. Right?"

Arnoni nodded and fell silent.

"Give him a sip of water. He has done well. I wouldn't want a dry throat to prevent him from continuing his song."

Noori sent one of the others to bring a glass down from the first floor and administer the liquid to Arnoni, whose hands were tied behind his back.

"Now I need you to tell me who these men were, Ponzio. Were they from inside my organization?"

"No. I didn't recognize the old fella."

"What about the other one then?"

Arnoni swallowed hard.

"Richard Cain."

"Is that who you work for?"

A nod. The blood fled from Alex's cheeks and a shiver ran down his spine. The tips of his fingers were cold, and he feared he might throw up.

"What do you want us to do with him, Alex?"

"Feed the farbissener momzer to the crows."

"Pardon?"

Alex took out a gun, forced it inside Arnoni's mouth, and pulled the trigger.

"It would have taken too long for me to explain, Noori."

25

ALEX RETURNED TO the States with Sarah and spent only one night before heading off to Chicago, leaving his wife to be near the family. He traveled to Cain's home and waited to find out what would happen. If Arnoni's confession was true, then Alex needed to have a quiet conversation about how Cain's loose talk almost cost him his life.

But Cain was nowhere to be seen. Judging by the mail sticking out of his post box, the fella hadn't been home for days, if not weeks. Alex waited half a block down the street in his rental, but he knew this would prove to be a colossal waste of time.

The guy had a small place downtown and that was Alex's next port of call. His was a long list of names in a serviced office with a large lobby and a disinterested security guard, so Alex hunkered down with a newspaper and a fresh pack of cigarettes.

His patience was paid back two hours later when Cain appeared and took the elevator up to the twelfth floor. Alex considered a visit but realized that the conversation he intended was best carried out away from any concerned citizen. So he would have to wait.

Four cigarettes later, Cain resurfaced. As soon as he had exited the building, Alex stood up and followed him. Cain walked three blocks west and two north before stopping outside Rosselli's diner. There he peered in through the windows, cupping his hand against the glass to remove the natural reflection and get a better view.

Whoever he was looking for must have been spotted, because he straightened up and marched inside. Alex crossed the road and tried to glimpse into the diner, but the only way to see the interior was to use Cain's method and he didn't want to be that direct.

Instead, he waited for Cain to sit down opposite his compadre and found that the fella had his back to the entrance. Alex chose the obvious solution to his problem, walked into the joint, and headed straight for the john.

He splashed some water on his face and dried his hands, just to give himself something to do to justify his arrival in the washroom. Then he popped out into the corridor and sauntered to the corner. Cain remained only ten feet away, but he had not seen a thing.

Alex sat behind him at the adjacent booth and leaned back to hear some of the conversation. Before he could get attuned to the voices, his waitress arrived and asked him what he wanted.

"A coffee, please."

"Is that all? You've got to order a meal at this time of day, mac."

"The house special then."

"You want fries with that?"

"Yes."

She craned to discern what Alex said as he tried not to be discovered by Cain in case the fella recognized his voice. All he achieved was to annoy the waitress because there was no way he could be heard over the general hubbub in the joint.

This meant he would have a hard time eavesdropping on his neighbors. Sure enough, Cain was inaudible because he faced away from Alex, but the other guy let slip sufficient volume that he picked up the overall tone of what they talked about.

"We'll need you to come downtown in the next day or so."

This snatch of conversation was almost all Alex needed. A bead of sweat dripped from his forehead to his lip, where he licked the salt off and grabbed a mouthful of coffee to take away the taste of his fear.

His waitress appeared with the special and he did his best to eat the chili presented to him. The flavor of the beef was off and there was so little heat to the bowl that it was hardly worth the effort to raise the spoon to his mouth.

Meantime, the two guys behind him were buried in hushed tones, which meant he had no clue what they were discussing. He threw down a healthy tip and left the joint, taking a position on the far side of the roadway.

Two cigarettes later and the men appeared, shook hands, and Cain headed east, while the other guy strode south. Alex guessed his destination almost before he set off, but he waited for confirmation. Sure enough, the flatfoot stopped on South Dearborn Street and entered the EM Dirksen building. He was a Fed.

ALEX LEANED AGAINST a wall, not wishing to believe what he had seen with his own eyes. Cain's lunch buddy was a G-Man, and there could only be one reason they would have been in conversation together. The respectful thing to do would be for Alex to travel to Mexico and visit Sam.

That way, he could ask permission to deal with the matter, but he couldn't be sure how long Cain and the Fed might dance around their handbags before the fella threw his chips in with the government cop. Then it would all be too late.

The other thing that was pretty obvious to Alex was that trailing the Fed would not tell him anything he didn't already know or had surmised. However, picking up Cain again might give him a chance to get a better idea of how far he'd got.

Alex turned tail and hopped a cab to Cain's office building, then sat in the lobby for another stint of the waiting game. Sure enough, less than an hour after arriving at his place of work, Cain went off for a second walkabout.

On this occasion, he left in the opposite direction to the diner. Down four blocks and over the road, Cain entered a bar and spent the time to sink one beer and speak to a guy with rolled-up sleeves.

Then back to the sidewalk and a brief journey south to bring Cain to a different diner. The same Fed as earlier sat in a booth and on this occasion Alex let them talk without eavesdropping. There was no point. Cain was in conversation with the flatfoot again and that indicated that he was getting ready to spill his guts.

Not for the first moment in his life, Alex decided that Sam Giancana's permission would have to wait. If Cain was taken in, then the fella would sing like a canary.

26

ALEX CONTINUED TO follow Cain that afternoon as the fella mooched from one place to the next. There was always a buddy to talk to and a drink to be downed. The guy traveled most of the south side, stopping off in one Italian cafe or another.

For somebody who was about to rat out his compadres, the man was in good humor. Alex waited for Cain to be alone long enough to whack him without witnesses, but the moment never came. The man spent the rest of the day in bars surrounded by large groups of men. And he was built like a camel and didn't hit the john once, despite the amount he had drunk.

The obvious plan B would be to follow him home and deal with him when he was in bed. Alex had to scrap even that idea when Cain left O'Flanagan's with a girl draped on his arm. Under ordinary circumstances, he would have taken them both out, but an unauthorized hit is one thing; murdering civilians at the same time would only bring down the wrath of the law.

Alex noted the address and then hustled over to his rental and perched four buildings from the skirt's entrance to await Cain's departure in the morning. Sure enough, the fella appeared around six. No breakfast and dawn cuddles for this guy. Instead, he hopped into a cab and scooted over to his apartment. This was the time for Alex to act, yet he did nothing.

In a moment of tremendous clarity, as he sat in his car waiting for Cain to shower and change, Alex came up with a new plan that was watertight. He pulled out a chunk of shrapnel from his case and headed to a phone booth to place an international call.

"GOOD TO HEAR your voice, Sam."

"Who is this?"

"An old friend from back home."

Silence on the line as Giancana did his best to recognize the stranger speaking to him. Then the penny dropped.

"I'm surprised that you've called me at all."

"In which case, you understand that this is important."

An audible sigh sounded from Giancana.

"What do you want?"

"There is someone close to you who is about to sing. I know who it is and where they are, but I need some help to finish the job."

"How long do we have?"

"I can't be precise, but I would expect today or tomorrow and before the end of the weekend, for sure."

More silence, but no huffing and puffing now.

"Where are you?"

"Chicago."

"I can put together a small group to support you in the next four hours."

Alex spotted a diner and named that as the meeting place.

"Should you tell me who it is?"

"On an open line, Sam?"

"Who?"

"Richard Cain."

"I understand. You are not seeking approval, are you?"

"The fella is about to sing his lungs out but I would like your consent if you're offering it."

Sam inhaled on a cigarette.

"Do you have proof?"

"I overheard him talking to a Fed."

"Permission granted."

"Thanks, Sam. I'll be in the coffee shop in four hours."

A GLANCE DOWN at his watch told Alex that the time was up. He waited in a back booth of the South Side Diner. At the exact right moment, three men entered the establishment and sauntered toward Alex.

"Hi, bud. Are these seats free?"

One of them was five inches taller than the others and the guy who stood next to him was a midget in comparison. The third was blond and of ordinary height. Alex remained silent until the shortest of the three looked skyward for a second.

"Yes, do sit down."

Once they had sorted themselves out, the tallest took charge.

"How do you know who we are?"

"Because I've been expecting three fellas like yourselves to appear storming through the door at the precise time that you lurched into view."

The midget smiled, and the blond nodded, and that was the moment the waitress came over to the booth and took their order. Coffee for everybody and a slice of cake each.

"This needs to be quick and clean. I have not come prepared for this job. We are reacting to circumstances as they unfold."

"We have brought some equipment."

Alex looked askance, and the blond explained: "In our saloon. It's parked in a lot a block away."

"Good. The mark is in his apartment and travels around the city either by foot or taxi. I have no itinerary to offer, but the target spends every waking minute in bars or a serviced building. Last night, he retired to a dame's pad and only taxied home to change. He traveled to his office half a block down from here. Until five minutes ago, he was still there."

The waitress approached with a tray and the blond issued a simple instruction.

"We'll have all that to go, miss."

Within a minute, they were on the sidewalk, heading west.

"What'll I call you fellas?"

"Larry, Curly, and Moe."

Larry was the tallest, Moe was blond, and Curly needed heels to hear what Larry said.

At Cain's building, Alex instructed Moe to check out the fella's floor and report back as soon as he could.

"Be back in ten, Pete."

The three remaining members of the party spread out in the lobby. Alex wished he'd brought another newspaper with him. Seven minutes later, Moe appeared and approached Alex first.

"He's in his office with a do not disturb sign hanging on the doorknob. Judging by the giggling and other noises, I'd say he is banging his secretary for a little while longer."

"You've got time to finish your cake then."

Moe shared the news with Larry and Curly, and the four fellas waited for Cain to wrap up his business upstairs.

THIRTY MINUTES AFTERWARD, Cain resurfaced and headed out of the joint. Alex and his three helpers exited and turned left. Two crossed to the other side of the street, while Curly and Alex stayed on the same sidewalk as Cain. Five blocks later and the mark popped into Rose's Sandwich Shop and the fellas huddled one building along.

"Shall we go in all guns blazing?"

"No, Curly. The aim is to avoid civilian casualties, but that doesn't mean we can't take advantage of the situation. Let's make it seem like a heist. Then we can whack the target in front of witnesses and it'll appear as though a robbery went wrong instead."

Larry nodded his approval and Moe whipped out a bunch of balaclavas, one for each man. They only popped them over their heads when they were outside the diner. At the same time, they pulled out their firearms from under their winter coats.

As soon as they entered the premises, Curly announced their arrival.

"This is a stickup. Don't any of you move and we'll be out of your way before you can blink."

The patrons raised their hands into the air and Curly instructed the girl at the cash till to empty its contents.

"We're almost done. All you have to do is take out any greenbacks from your wallets and watches from your wrists."

To facilitate this procedure, the fellas made everyone stand in a row facing a far wall. Cain was a third of the way along the line from the right and Alex took his position near Giancana's capo.

Moe started at the left and threw the cash he collected into his bag, and half the time he gave up trying to grab at the wristwatches. He turned to the waitress, who had opened the register. "You gotta get a better quality of customer, lady. Most of their timepieces aren't worth stealing."

"Stop giving business advice and let's get this done."

Alex feigned annoyance to divert attention away from their actual task. When Moe reached Cain, the guy handed over a large handful of gelt but refused to turn over his gold watch.

Alex stepped forward and placed the barrel of his shotgun at Cain's head and let Moe continue to do the talking.

"Don't be a fool. Hand it over and we'll be out of your hair."

Cain shook his head and Alex poked his ear with the gun, but the watch remained on his wrist.

"Last chance, buddy."

As soon as Moe's words left his lips, Alex squeezed the trigger, and a sea of red splattered against the wall. Two women stood next to Cain screamed as bits of his head landed on their clothes and hair.

Moe leaned down and put another slug in Cain's skull before undoing the watch strap and adding it to the pile in his bag.

"We are done here. Merry Christmas everyone."

Larry, Curly, and Moe joined Alex as he stormed out of the coffee shop and ran down the street. Into their car and Larry drove as fast and as far away from Rose's as he could until they reached the outskirts of the city.

"Thank you for your help, gentlemen. Feel free to share the cash among you, but I need hardly remind you to take care if you sell those watches."

"We understand. Would you like us to dispose of your shotgun?"

"No disrespect, but I always handle that matter myself."

"Fine by me. Can we drop you anywhere?"

"Let me break this gun into several pieces. Then take me to the airport."

May 1975

27

ALEX AND SARAH savored their time together over the next couple of years. They joined a local golf club and enjoyed the days they spent with their extended family. He did his best to put his assassination of Richard Cain behind him, but the memory never faded from the back of Alex's mind.

"Sarah, before I divest my Vegas interests, at last, I need to be certain that when I do, there is no chance the mob'll come calling one day."

"Massimo and Ezra will be pleased to hear you talk about this again."

"They get paid enough not to complain. I've already reduced the size of my cut twice in the last couple of years."

"Alex, you know what I mean. You've been promising them you'd relinquish control for longer than the lives of our grandchildren. Those two won't wait forever."

"One step at a time. Right now, I'm more concerned about the commission. Handing over assets can't help me if some Italian fires a bullet in my skull."

Sarah stared at him and rubbed some moisture out of her right eye.

"I'm sorry, but those two must wait a little longer. My higher priority is to make sure I am not on the commission's radar."

"And how are you going to do that? It's not like you can attend a meeting and ask them."

Alex smiled.

"No, but I could do the next best thing and speak to Sam Giancana. He is about the only Italian mobster I can speak to nowadays."

"Is this a long-winded way of telling me you are on another trip to Mexico?"

"Not at all, Sarah. I read in the papers he returned to the US a while ago. Chicago is my destination."

THE CONCESSIONS AT O'Hare Airport might be different, but Alex found his way out of the terminal building with no trouble. He hadn't been to the Windy City since the Cain hit, in stark contrast to the glory days of Prohibition. Alfonse Capone was long dead, and Alex had no desire to join him.

After three changes of cab en route from his hotel, he was still forced to walk a further six blocks with a layoff in a store every minute. These were the rules for an audience with Giancana now that he was back from Mexico, but desperate to lie low. Alex popped into an Italian cafe and waited at the entrance to be seated.

"Do you have a special booth for me near the kitchen?"

The maître d' nodded and he followed the guy up a set of steps to the rear of the establishment, along a corridor, and into a private room. As Alex stepped in, the door was closed tight behind him.

"Good to see you, Sam. Thanks for agreeing to this meet."

"The pleasure is all mine, Alex. Would you like a drink or something to eat?"

"A mugful would be great. Is there any cheesecake?"

Sam rang a bell, and a waiter arrived, vanished, and then, a couple of minutes later reappeared with a pot of coffee and cheesecake.

"Enough with the small talk, Alex. Why do you feel the urge to visit me after all these years? I should warn you now, if you are hoping to wallow in nostalgia you've come to the wrong place."

Alex lit a cigarette and took a sip of his coffee.

"Even before the unfortunate accident which befell Richard Cain, I've been concerned about my relationship with our Italian friends. If I'm to remain safe in my retirement, then I need to know no one has any interest in coming after me. I want to be sure that part of my past is long gone and will not resurface."

"I understand your concern, Alex, but you have visited the wrong man."

Alex took a bite of his cheesecake.

"Ever since that terrible business with the grand jury and my subsequent departure to Mexico, I've been out of the commission."

"But I expected—"

"It doesn't mean I am without influence though my control of this town waned in my absence. But I want you to appreciate I do not have a vote and none of them invite me to speak at their meetings."

"Sam, that's as may be, but I've got to know. Are they still after me because of Bobby Kennedy?"

"First, don't utter his name in my presence. Second, all I can say for sure is that when I was last in discussions with the commission, you did not come up. Nobody was looking to whack you then. Have you done anything to change that opinion?"

"Not that I am aware."

"You are probably safe then."

"That's not good enough. I need to be certain."

"Don't we all, Alex. What did you use to say?"

"We live together, we love together, but we die alone."

"And that's all you can be sure of in this life. Anything else is clover."

Alex took a long drag on his cigarette and sat in silence as he consumed the cheesecake.

"How are you faring, Sam?"

"I'm doing all right. I maintain my interests in several operations, but they don't let me anywhere near the big deals anymore."

"Aren't you concerned about the number of rats that are surfacing?"

"In my day, we would have cut out their tongues and left them dying in the street for the others to see. Then the chance of a second canary in the organization was much reduced."

"We'd have whacked the Fed they spoke with too."

"Times were easier when we had greater influence on law enforcement, Alex."

"Ever had the desire to leave all this behind you?"

"I've known too many people and been involved in far too much to walk away. The most I hope for is to live out the rest of my days in peace."

"Is that your way of telling me if the trail is cold enough, then I shouldn't need to worry?"

"Alex, I am issuing no instructions to you whatsoever. All I know is that the commission will only take action against those who jeopardize it. If you do not threaten to rat them out or put a hit out on a member of the mob, then I can't see why they will care whether you live or die, to be honest."

"And what happened with your grand jury escapade?"

"I refused to rat anyone out and fled the country."

"There was talk you'd cut a deal."

"If it were true, then I'd either be dead or in witness protection."

Alex nodded.

"In my experience, Alex, you will never get the certainty you crave, but you can get close by severing anybody who ties you to your criminal life. And be ruthless with anyone you suspect might sing."

"Sam, you aren't taking your own advice though."

"Oh?"

"I'm still alive, and what we both know could take us to the gas chamber and beyond."

"What we have, Alex, is an unspoken understanding. If you rat me out, you won't draw breath on the first day of the trial. If you squeal, then it'll be the last thing you ever do."

"Straight back at you, Sam."

"I know, which is why we can trust each other."

28

WHEN ALEX ARRIVED back home from Chicago, he found Moishe, Alecia and Oscar in his living room.

"How are things with you guys?"

"All good, Pop. Have you been on another one of your trips?"

"Yes, I like to keep in touch with some of my old friends from out of town."

"Wouldn't it have been easier to phone, Alex?"

"Alecia, I'm not much of a telephone fella. I prefer to meet people face-to-face when I speak with them."

"I suppose there are things you don't want to talk about on an open line."

Alex glared at her for a second, trying to decide what she knew and what she didn't. Moishe must have read his father's face.

"Did you have a good time while you were on vacation, Pop?"

Alex turned his attention to his son and away from his wife.

"Moishe, the problem with seeing people from your past is that nostalgia places a veil over your memory. So the fella appeared way too old for my liking, but when we talked, it was like we'd just seen each other the day before."

"None of us are getting any younger, Pop."

"Ain't that the truth?"

Sarah entered, followed by Veronica with a tray.

"We didn't hear you come in, Alex. Veronica, please would you get another cup?"

The housekeeper hustled out of the room in search of more crockery, while Sarah poured drinks from a large pot.

"When we were kids, we'd have been sitting around the kitchen for only a coffee and a slice of cake."

"A lot has happened since you were a boy, Moishe. We used to live in an apartment in midtown New York, and now look at us."

His mother grinned from ear to ear.

"Sarah, that was quite a swanky joint. The places we lived before the kids were born; they were in the depths of the Bowery; those were skanky."

"My point still stands, Pop. We've gone upmarket."

Alex smiled at how far his relationship with Moishe had traveled over the years. As a kid, he was so certain that his father was evil personified that he would have nothing to do with him. Now he took care of Alex's financial affairs. The legitimate ones, at any rate.

"My boy, I do not apologize for looking after my family and helping you all to have a better life in this country. If I embarrassed you by eating cheesecake in here, then you are welcome to sit in the kitchen if it makes you happier."

Moishe looked at Alex for a second and then laughed.

"You got me."

Alecia sat stony-faced, not seeing the joke. A moment later she stood up and left the room.

ONCE VERONICA CLEARED away the snacks, Moishe joined Alex as he unpacked from his trip, leaving the women and grandson to head to the patio. With a shirt in his hand, he began his interrogation.

"Are you happy with Alecia?"

"Yes, Pop. Why do you ask all of a sudden?"

"Something she mentioned earlier that caught my attention. It'll be nothing, for sure."

Moishe mulled over Alex's comment.

"What was it she said?"

"Alecia spoke about my line of business and implied I was involved in some form of criminal enterprise. We both know how I have earned my money, so that is not my issue. What worries me is where she got the idea from. Have you discussed my investments with her?"

"Not at all, Pop. A long time ago, I told you I didn't name my clients in front of her, and that accounting was so dull to her she never asked me about my business. That hasn't changed. If she got ideas in her head about your past, then she did not get them from me."

"Moishe, that is what I believed, but I prefer to check these things than let them fester. That is how resentment builds, and you and I are better than that."

Alex rolled up some unused socks and placed them in a drawer.

"So, you and Alecia are happy then?"

"You just asked me that, Pop."

"I know, but you have only one kid, so a father may wonder if his son is content with so few heirs."

"Don't start this again. We are all fine and I reconciled myself years ago to the fact that we would not be as blessed as David and Dorit."

"Now you sound like a rabbi."

Moishe grinned.

"No danger of that, but I know you'd wish for as many grandkids as possible. Mama especially."

"Of course, but I am more concerned about your happiness than the number of…"

Alex's voice trailed off, and he stared out of the window. He dropped his socks on the floor and headed out of the bedroom.

"Call David. Now."

By the time he was halfway down the stairs, the doorbell rang.

"No one answer that door."

Veronica had appeared from the kitchen and Sarah was in the hallway too. Both women stopped in their tracks at Alex's instruction.

"What…?"

"Leave this to me, Sarah."

Alex took a deep breath and opened the front door to find three flatfeet flashing their badges at him.

"Federal Agent Bradigan. May we come in?"

All three were dressed in the traditional Fed uniform of gray suit, white shirt, blue tie, shiny black shoes, and haircuts that screamed out G-Man.

"Do you have a warrant to enter the premises?"

Bradigan turned to the guy next to him, who stuffed his hand into his inside jacket pocket and came out with bupkis. Alex laughed.

"They've sent boys to do men's work. Come back when you've found a judge who'll approve of you bothering me and my family. Until then, *zoygn meyn hon*."

DAVID ARRIVED AS the Feds pulled out of the driveway.

"What the hell just happened?"

"I was going to ask you the same question, David."

"On what grounds did they want to search the premises?"

"They had no paperwork, David. I'll guess they can find a judge and they will be back."

Everybody stood in the hallway except Alecia, who only now appeared on the scene. She screamed on hearing Alex's words and collapsed to the floor. Moishe ran over to comfort her as Alex glanced down at the blubbering a few feet away.

"Let's all keep our heads clear. Nothing has happened yet. Sarah, is there anything in this building that might need to be filed someplace else in the next thirty minutes?"

His wife shook her head.

"David, will a warrant for the house cover the office buildings on the same grounds?"

"Unlikely. That'd only work if the Feds knew what they were looking for. I mean, if they had something specific in mind, then they would cast the net wide to be sure to get it. The fact they forgot their paperwork indicates this was more about harassment than law enforcement. I can file a suit in the morning if you want me to."

"One thing at a time, David. Let's all go about whatever it is we were doing. I still need to finish unpacking, and that is what I intend to do."

Alex glanced at Alecia, who remained on the floor.

"Moishe, you might prefer to take Alecia and Oscar home in case there is any more excitement this afternoon."

"I'm fine, Alex. It was the shock of it all. I've never experienced anything like this in my life and you all seem so calm."

Sarah smiled. "This isn't the first time a government agency has tried to search my home, Alecia. If you had lived the childhood that Alex and I grew up in, then you would understand why this doesn't register on our scale of concern."

Her husband helped Alecia get to her feet, and they moved into the living room. With a nod from Sarah, Veronica offered everyone a fresh cup of coffee and Alex went upstairs. Back in the bedroom, he picked up his socks from the floor and continued to unpack. Sarah came in with a coffee in her hand.

"I expect you might need this."

"Thanks."

"Do you reckon it was a fishing expedition?"

"Not really, but I needed to get Alecia to relax."

"She's not used to this side of our family life."

"The woman let slip enough hints earlier on though. Does she know about my past?"

"You believe she dropped a dime to the Feds?"

"It has already crossed my mind, Sarah. What was all that business about my line of work over the cheesecake?"

"Alecia read it in the paper over the weekend. One of the Sunday newspapers ran a piece on which criminals from the old days were alive and well in Miami-Dade. You were on the list."

Alex zipped up his now-empty case and sat on the bed.

"The press are still bothering to write about me? I haven't been in the public eye since the height of Cuba."

"It wasn't Alecia, Alex. We can trust her."

He stood up and hugged his wife.

"Sarah, let's check every room for firearms. If those vermin come back, they shouldn't find any weapons here."

"Into the vault they go, Alex."

29

THE FEDS DIDN'T return, but everybody remained shaken for several days. Alex found it hard to take his doubts about Alecia out of his mind too, but he did his best. After all, the woman could read about him in the papers, despite his reservations about her commitment to the family.

"Do you expect we've seen the last of the cops, Alex?"

"It's unlikely, Sarah. The G-Men are like mold; once it gets hold, it's impossible to get rid of."

"You and Meyer used to call them cockroaches."

"We weren't wrong, but before the war, they had little support. Now every politician under the sun wants to be seen to be fighting the mob. It's their way of demonstrating they are tough on crime."

"While taking a brown envelope full of green."

"So it has been, so it is, and how it will be long after we've all turned to dust."

"And have you got off Alecia, Alex?"

"I'm doing my best, but this recent incident is not the only time I've questioned her loyalty."

"Or is this just your way of saying Moishe could have done better for himself?"

"Sarah, I am not suggesting anything of the sort, but as you're bringing it up."

"Don't drag me into your web of family intrigue. She might be too much of a Jewish princess for my taste, but Alecia makes our son happy."

"And that is more than I could ever do, Sarah."

"Now who's putting words into my mouth?"

"If only she'd get pregnant again."

"Alex, stop. Not everyone can and not everybody wants to have a brood of children. Moishe seems to have made his peace with the situation and so should you."

"I like the woman, but almost every time we meet, she makes some barbed comments and I don't appreciate them."

"It's the princess oozing out. Alecia tries her best to hide it, but that side of her personality is never far from the surface. Moishe sucks it in, so we must too. It is not our problem, Alex."

"My business is the safety and security of this family, and if Alecia threatens the stability of that, then I will stick my nose in their affairs."

"Alex, we are a long way from that. Separate how you feel about Moishe's wife from the fact Alecia has done nothing to harm any member of the family. In fact, she does us an enormous good by keeping Moishe in check and content. Imagine what he'd be like without her calming influence?"

Alex shuddered as he recalled the teenage version of his son who had shunned him for so many years.

"You should tell her to cut out the snide remarks about my past. I don't appreciate them and they don't make her appear good in anyone's eyes, not least Moishe's."

"I'll pass on the message, Alex."

AFTER BREAKFAST, ALEX and Sarah moved back indoors because there was a chill in the air. Veronica made another pot of coffee and left them alone in the kitchen.

"Do you have any idea why the Feds visited us, Alex?"

“I’ve been racking my brains ever since they tried to set foot in here. There’s nothing I have done to lead them to start an investigation. Nothing new, that is.”

He stared at Sarah to head off her comment before it even formed inside her mind.

“And that’s why you believe there must be a rat? In the family?”

“The Feds had a reason to believe they could walk in here and find something incriminating. Apart from a couple of revolvers, there’s nothing I know of to cause us any concern. So that leaves a canary.”

“But who, Alex?”

“My best guess was Alecia, as you know. If it wasn’t her, and I accept that’s the situation, then we are left either with somebody on the outskirts of our affairs who knows nothing but can big themselves up to escape a beef with the authorities…”

“Or someone very close indeed.”

“Right, Sarah. We’re talking about one of our kids, their wives, Veronica, or the lieutenants. I can’t imagine anyone else who fits the profile.”

“Alex, are you telling me you think it is one of those people? Our closest allies?”

“No, not at all, but it is my current line of thinking. A rat at the center of the operation or some old situation that has come home to roost.”

“Like what, Alex?”

“Tito, maybe. Despite what I said and believed, I’m not sure I got to the bottom of the extent of his spying on us.”

“He lied to get himself over to Florida, but it doesn’t make him a rat.”

“No, that is true.”

Alex pondered the same problem again as they both consumed their coffees. Sarah rummaged in the refrigerator and took out some cheesecake.

“The other unresolved situation was Liddy.”

He peered into Sarah’s eyes as she spoke those words.

“What do you mean?”

"Exactly what I say. You told me the mob was behind her death as a warning to you, but you didn't sound convinced then. Have you changed your mind since?"

"It was murder for sure, not an accidental overdose, but I've no clearer idea now than back then who did for her."

Sarah sighed. There was a weariness in her expression which made Alex swallow.

"You were with her for quite some time, Alex."

"I know. If she'd been any other actress, then she would still be alive today."

"Alex, you told me she was no one special to you. Just a young woman who was willing to sleep with you."

He stared down into his lap.

"Liddy looked like Rebecca to me."

It was Sarah's turn to freeze.

"You never mentioned that detail, Alex. Why hide it from me?"

"I was embarrassed and I'm ashamed, even now."

"Alex, I've told you before. Your infidelities don't hurt me as much as your lies about them. That ended our first marriage. Did I care you were carrying on with some drug-fiend ex-actress? Not especially, but every time I asked you, there was a pathetic pretense that nothing was happening. And we both knew it wasn't true."

Alex lit a cigarette and inhaled deeply.

"I assumed you'd think less of me because Liddy reminded me of Rebecca."

"Are you trying to tell me, Alex, I must compete with that woman even though she has been in her grave for decades?"

"Sarah, there is no competition. The actress looked like Rebecca. I was weak and foolish, and that is the long and the short of it."

"You don't get to wriggle off the hook that easy, Alex. You could gaze at the girl from afar. There was no need to build an annex to the offices so you could tryst with her. That shows much more interest than the fact she appeared a little like your dead girlfriend."

Alex winced.

"Have you got to the point when you have nothing to say to me?"

She glared at him.

"You need to find somewhere else to sleep for the next few weeks, Alex. I'm angry with you and I hope it will abate, but I will not lie to you. I don't know what's going to happen to us."

30

TO KEEP SOME distance between Sarah and himself, Alex hopped over to Palm Springs to continue the dialogue about him handing over the reins of the Vegas operation. He had considered spending time with Meyer, but he knew that this thorny problem needed resolution.

Yet another afternoon with Alex, Massimo, and Ezra in the kitchen of the second home. The tense silence made Alex remind himself why he hadn't just taken a short drive and visited Meyer on the other side of Miami. His friend had been thrown out of Israel and returned to the US. Having dodged the bullet of the federal trial, Lansky was attempting to live a quiet life.

Instead, Alex stared at his lieutenants as Massimo stirred his drink. A flashback memory to the Bowery and the first day they had met. He was a petulant kid who had only moved over to Alex's gang when Charlie Lucky demanded it. Sixty years later and they continued to share a mug of coffee, and Massimo still didn't take cream.

"Did you read what's happened in Cambodia?"

The two lieutenants shrugged in ignorance and disinterest.

"The war in Vietnam may be over, but there remains trouble in Asia."

"Alex, with all due respect, why should we worry?"

"Ezra, keeping on top of what is going on in the world is not a bad thing, especially when it impacts what happens at home."

"The Vegas take has remained steady. What else is there to care about?"

Massimo stared at Alex and then looked at his coffee before swigging down a large glug.

"You guys slay me. There are opportunities out there for the taking if you'd raise your eyes beyond the Vegas horizon."

"Alex, that is easy for you to say, but our fortune and our survival are tied to that city and a handful of casinos. We don't have the luxury that you do. We scrabble in the dirt every day to make gelt for you."

"Ezra, my cut has been only a tithe for several years. The rest has been yours to do with what you want. The choice has been for you to invest in other business ventures or put your money in real estate to house your mistresses. I do not judge what you do with your wealth, but please don't imply that you haven't been rewarded well for your significant effort. That goes for you too, Massimo."

Alex ground his molars at the way the fellas were behaving, as though he was responsible for all their woes. These grown men were acting like they were teenagers again in the rear of the Bowery's Forsyth Hotel.

ALEX DECIDED THE best thing to do was to walk away from the two gonifs who were annoying him, so he stepped out onto the patio and lit a cigarette. His lieutenants read the situation well and stayed indoors. Ezra and Massimo only appeared when he stubbed out the smoke.

"It has been a tough couple of years, Alex."

"Yes, Massimo. For all of us, I'd say. My attempts to separate myself from my criminal past are a continual struggle. Meanwhile, you fellas worked hard to keep the wheels on the bus when I guess you'd wanted to sit behind the wheel of the vehicle and drive off into the sunset."

"Pretty much, Alex."

He nodded at Ezra's honesty and sighed. Alex knew they were right, and that he was holding back from handing over control.

"Alex, we want to negotiate with you over the terms of a transfer of ownership of the Vegas casinos."

"Ezra, I understand. What do you propose?"

"You hand over power as soon as possible, but we maintain your remuneration for a further twelve months. At that point, we'll make a final payment in full settlement of the assets of fifty million."

Alex's left eye twitched for a second. Although this was a large sum offered to him, in the grand scheme of things, it didn't sound big enough. Half a year's take? Was that all he was worth to them? To avoid responding, he lit another smoke.

"What do you reckon?"

"Massimo, you must give me a moment to consider my position. On the one hand, Sarah and I could live off that final payout for the rest of our days, but on the other, it represents six months' income, which is not a huge amount given how many decades I have put into the casino business."

Ezra glanced at Massimo, who waited a second before replying.

"The lump sum is a token, Alex. It is not intended to represent fair value for the forward cash flow of all the Vegas casinos under your influence. Instead, we view it as an acknowledgment that what you are giving us is a substantial foothold into the commission and an income stream that'll last beyond our lifetimes."

Ezra added his ten cents.

"Besides, Alex, you've extracted tremendous value out of Vegas gaming over the years. You demonstrated that when you agreed to reduce your take from the skim down to eleven percent."

Alex walked back inside to make a pot of coffee and Massimo followed him in.

"We're not trying to hustle you, Alex."

"I know that, Massimo, but if I transfer the casinos over to you, then I will have nothing."

"When, not if, Alex."

"When I hand them over."

Alex boiled water and bustled around the stove until there was steaming brown liquid bubbling in the pot.

"You were saying, Alex?"

"Was I, Massimo?"

The lieutenant shrugged and wandered back outside to have a quick word with Ezra. As soon as Alex arrived, they stopped talking and stared at him again. He sat down and took a sip of his fresh brew.

"We don't want to argue with you about gelt."

"Pleased to hear it, Ezra."

"But that doesn't mean we agree with you. The terms we are offering are more than fair, especially when you consider how patient we've been with you. We have waited since your return from Cuba. I think that was when you mentioned you would hand over Vegas to us."

"More or less, Ezra. It has been a long time and I am the first to admit that."

"Too long, Alex. Cuba was twenty years ago, and here we still are."

"Not quite, Massimo, but I get your point."

"Fifty million after a year, so there is a clear transition and to let every Italian family know that we are the people to deal with."

"That has been the case for a few years, Ezra."

"I know, Alex, but what you haven't been party to are the considerable questions we get over whether you are still involved and the extent you oversee each gaming house."

Yet another cigarette sparked into life in Alex's hand.

"What if today is not the right time?"

"If not now, then when, Alex?"

He opened his mouth to reply and then thought better of it. Ezra filled the void.

"If we don't reach an agreement by July fourth, then we will need to go off on our own, Alex."

A deep drag on his smoke and he pondered the threat that his lieutenant had just issued with a calm voice and an icy heart.

"What would you do?"

"There is an appetite to form a consortium in Vegas and pool skim operations. It would reduce a chunk of overhead and the mob bosses seem open to the idea."

"You've already spoken to the commission on this, Massimo?"

"Let's just say we've made overtures. Nothing has been confirmed. Nothing has been agreed, but if a smooth handover between us doesn't happen, then you will force us to consider our other options."

"And we both assert this with all due respect, Alex."

31

ALEX CAME HOME, chastened by his time spent with Ezra and Massimo. He rang the doorbell and Veronica appeared. She glanced at him for a second, then walked back to the kitchen, leaving him to enter the house on his own. No greeting, no smile—Sarah told her what had happened.

He dropped his bags in the hall and ventured into the living room but his wife was not there. A head bobbed from outside and he stepped onto the patio.

"I hope you'll let me stay here again, Sarah."

"Enough time has elapsed that my anger at you has passed. I've not forgiven you, Alex, but I can stand the sight of you now."

He swallowed hard and thanked her. Then he sat down and, a few minutes later, the housekeeper appeared with a pot of coffee and one mug.

"Please get something for Alex. He is back from his trip and is home with us."

"Shall I prepare a spare room, Sarah?"

Alex looked at his wife.

"There's no need for that, Veronica."

He sighed with relief. At least Sarah was prepared to welcome him into her bed again. The housekeeper raised her eyes and returned with a second mug, which she almost threw at him. Then she vanished into the house.

"You've not won any friends there, Alex."

"True, but I'll survive if Veronica is annoyed with me."

"Big talk for a man whose food is going to be spat on every day this week."

He raised the corner of his mouth and was about to respond but chose silence instead.

"Let's spend today in each other's company, Alex, and we'll pick apart our relationship tomorrow."

THAT AFTERNOON, THE two remained on the patio, soaking in the rays of the sun and talking about everything and nothing at all.

"How concerned are you that Massimo and Ezra are about to go their own way?"

"Ezra has always been interested in furthering his own interests. Massimo was more loyal."

"That doesn't answer my question, Alex."

"You're right, possibly because I don't know. As far as they are concerned, I've been dangling them on a line for years and they've had it up to here."

Alex's flat hand touched his throat.

"And if they do not get what I promised, then they have every reason to go elsewhere. I don't blame them, but I wish they could be more patient."

"The world doesn't follow the beat of your drum, Alex."

"No, but they are chasing after ever more money. To me, that's a waste of energy, because they must own more than enough for a comfortable life from now until their dying days."

"Alex, what about the possibility that it isn't gelt they are after, but something else?"

"Like what, Sarah?"

"Power, prestige, respect. They've spent their entire lives working for you. Sounds to me as though they want a taste of being top dog."

He lit a cigarette.

"You're right, as ever. They fund a lifestyle that encompasses their families and at least one mistress a piece. And both fellas still flash cash to splash. They are not chasing greenbacks."

Sarah smiled, leaned her head back on her seat, and closed her eyes.

"For a clever man, you aren't very bright sometimes, Alex."

HE CAME DOWNSTAIRS from emptying his bags and putting his things away. He popped into the kitchen, but nobody was there. Out to the patio and Sarah remained where he had left her.

"Where's Veronica?"

"I gave her the night off. She needs to wrap her head around the fact that you remain in my life."

"Was she hoping that she had seen the back of me?"

"Maybe. She offered me scissors to cut up your suits."

He nodded and made a mental note to ensure he was not left alone with the woman for a while. He didn't need to be given a hard time by a housekeeper.

"Did any survive?"

"I turned down her suggestion."

"Thank you."

"Alex, if I was looking to destroy your clothes, I wouldn't wait for Veronica to give me a weapon."

"That's one of the many things I like about you."

She smiled.

"What did you want with her anyway?"

"I was only going to ask her what was for dinner."

"We could take out or I could rustle something up if you prefer?"

"Why don't we go to a restaurant? We haven't been out to eat for ages."

"Aren't you still concerned about getting hit?"

"Of course, but I was an easier mark in Palm Springs than here."

"How so?"

"I stayed in one place the entire time I was there. If somebody had a contract out on me, they'd have executed it in the house."

THEY ONLY POPPED into a local restaurant in the center of town. Nothing fancy but Falco's served good quality fare at a reasonable price. Sarah took the sea bass and Alex chose steak and fries, as he always did when he went out to eat.

"Don't you ever get bored with having the same thing?"

"It may come with the same name, but every joint serves the meal differently and the recipes invariably contain a wide variety of ingredients. And anyway, if they can't cook a steak properly, then there's no point being in the restaurant."

"After all these years, you can still surprise me. I assumed it was because you couldn't be bothered to read the menu."

"Sarah, there is that consideration too. You're right that I am a creature of habit."

He smiled, and they clinked wine glasses. She knew him too well sometimes. Conversation twisted and turned during the meal, and the couple circled around the topic of Liddy without ever arriving at it. Alex didn't possess the energy to discuss his indiscretion in the middle of a restaurant, and he hoped Sarah was so minded.

WITH A COFFEE in front of them and an empty plate where there was once a piece of cheesecake, she opened up a fresh line of conversation.

"We haven't talked about why you made me so angry."

Alex swallowed but understood they had unfinished business to discuss.

"I shouldn't have told you the details about what attracted me to Liddy. It was unnecessary to rub your face in it and I gave you too much information. I believed I was being honest and open, but now I realize it was vindictive and hurtful. Sorry, Sarah."

"I accept your apology, but your words mean little. You are still embroiled with the mob, and that is the source of all your problems, wouldn't you say?"

"What do you mean? The mob had nothing to do with Liddy's death."

"First, Alex, you don't know that's true. You said yourself that the girl was murdered and her overdose was faked. Second, Vegas is on the edge of collapse. Massimo and Ezra have stood between you and the Italians in that town for far too long."

"It's been hard to let go, Sarah."

"So you've been saying all these years, Alex."

"Do you think I've been lying?"

"Only to yourself, Alex. If you wanted to get out, then you would have. I can't recall a single occasion in your life when you did anything you didn't want to."

He mulled over Sarah's comment. Perhaps she was right. He had been talking about letting go for a lifetime and still he owned the Vegas connections.

"I've said this to you before, Alex, but it all boils down to trust."

"What do you mean?"

"All that binds us together are the words we speak and the actions we perform. But if you keep repeating the same mantra and do nothing afterward, then you shouldn't be surprised if people respond."

"Do you believe I should hand over to Ezra and Massimo?"

"For sure, before they do something you'll regret. And if you want me to believe you in the future, then you must do what you say. Talk is too cheap in this world."

He lit another cigarette and inhaled the smoke deep inside his lungs.

"Alex, if I am to trust you, then be true to your word."

"Two indiscretions in forty years, Sarah."

"Both times, it's been you with an actress and the only reason you met them in the first place was because of the life you've lived. The things you call investments are killing you, and I will not sit here and watch you do that to yourself."

He swallowed.

"Either you free yourself from the shackles of Vegas, or I won't be with you anymore, Alex."

32

WHEN ALEX WOKE up the next morning, Sarah had already gone downstairs. He smelled coffee and his stomach rumbled. Time to get up, so he showered and got dressed. He stared out of the bedroom window and reminisced about the mobsters he'd known. Almost all of them, to a man, were dead. In contrast, the center of his world was his wife and their family.

He threw some clothes on and padded down to the kitchen. Sarah poured him a drink as he walked into the room.

"I reckon it would be nice for us to eat on the patio this morning."

He smiled and gave her a peck on the cheek while making sure not to spill his coffee. Alex peered out and watched the sun in the sky. He imagined the warmth on his face and he took his drink outside along with the paper Sarah had placed on the kitchen table.

When he sat out on the patio, an image on the front of the newspaper leaped out at him; hordes of Vietnamese civilians desperate to reach the inside of an American helicopter. Saigon was in tatters and the US was fleeing with its tail between its legs.

Sarah's eyes flitted onto the photo as she sat down and he contemplated the differences between his experience in the trenches of France and modern warfare.

"I can't imagine what it must be like fighting in the jungles of Vietnam, Sarah."

"Does this bring it all back?"

Alex nodded and held her hand. They'd given him a Purple Heart for killing a kid who pinned down what was left of his platoon. If that was all it took to win a medal in Asia, the entire Marine corps would be weighed down with pieces of metal attached to their chests. Everything had gone downhill since Kennedy was assassinated. He shuddered.

"Let's not dwell in the past, Alex. Just fix on the idea that we live together, we love together, but we die alone."

"I know. I guess I'm sad that it has come to this." He flicked the newspaper. "America was supposed to be the land of milk and honey when we arrived at Ellis Island. Instead, it has sent tens of thousands of boys off to be slaughtered and broadcast pictures home every night to show us what is being done in our name."

"Alex, you almost sound concerned. I assumed your concerns were limited to our family and your business interests."

"Most of the time, but now and again…"

He lost himself in his thoughts once more. What had this country become? He was glad his parents were dead, so they weren't forced to witness what was going on. Meanwhile, Sarah topped up his mug and passed him a cigarette she'd lit. He sucked on the smoke to drag his lungs into the present day and with the next two tokes, the rest of his body followed.

Alex turned the page and scanned for more positive headlines. By the time he'd reached the centerfold, Sarah had brought out his breakfast. He stubbed out the butt of his cigarette and smiled at his wife.

"Thank you."

Cereal, smoked salmon bagel, and cheese blintzes along with a glass of juice to go with his coffee. Just the way he liked it.

He chewed through the bagel first and after that, he felt better.

HE PUT DOWN his silverware and took the last glug from his mug.

"That was good. Thank you again, but where's Veronica? Shouldn't she be making the breakfasts around here?"

Sarah chuckled.

"We gave the housekeeper the day off, don't you recall?"

He stared at her. When had that happened? This business with Sarah and Vegas had rattled his brain.

"That way, we could spend some time alone together."

That made sense, but Alex's cheeks glowed and he stared at his lap in shame.

"I have been a disappointment to you for so long, Sarah."

"Don't talk like that, Alex Cohen. Yes, you've made some mistakes along the way, but you also did your best to be a good father to our children and a provider to this family."

"Will you ever forgive me?"

"I told you I have done so already. If I had not, you wouldn't be sitting at this table. You'd still be back in Palm Springs. Let's not rehash old arguments. What's done is done and we have the rest of our lives to look forward to. Together."

"Thank you, Sarah."

"Remember, Alex, that if you can't move past this, we will never be happy again. You must acknowledge to yourself what you did and accept the past for what it is. I know I am doing my best to, and you must do so too."

Sarah was right, as ever. He was surprised at how forgiving she was, but over the years she'd learned that men do stupid things despite themselves. You can accept or not. She accepted him for who he was but needed to know that he'd stop putting himself in situations where he might chase tail rather than follow his heart.

He stood up from the breakfast table and gave her a kiss on the lips.

"I must sort out my affairs."

Then he wandered off to his workroom on the other side of the pool.

INSIDE THE SUMMERHOUSE, Alex sat in front of his desk and dialed a number.

"Can you do me a favor and not go into the office today?"

"Sure, Pop. But why?"

"David, there's some work I wish you to do for me and I need us to focus on it with no interruptions, even from Moishe."

"There's nothing I had planned that can't wait twenty-four hours."

"I'll pick you up in thirty minutes."

Alex grabbed his briefcase and tossed out a bunch of papers onto the floor. Then he sighed, knowing that was unnecessary behavior, and picked up the pages and threw them in the trashcan next to the desk.

He rifled through the drawers until he found a Manila file and shoved that in the case. Then he sat back and lit a cigarette, enjoying the moment of calm he had created for himself. Up on his feet, out of the summerhouse and over to Sarah, who was smoking next to an empty table.

Alex smiled, kissed her goodbye, and walked out the front door. The car was still out in front of the garage, where he'd left it the day before. He had yet to get used to the fact that Tito wasn't available to park the car under cover. Perhaps they should hire a chauffeur or handyman to potter around and fix things. He'd mention the idea to Sarah.

With his case on the passenger seat beside him, he turned the motor over, but nothing. He sighed. *Damn jalopy*. Alex took a deep breath and tried again.

The engine spluttered into life and sparks flashed out of the dashboard. Acting on instinct alone, he flung his entire weight on the driver's door and pushed himself out of the vehicle, just as an explosion burst around him and threw him onto the ground. Before the gravel slammed into his face, everything went black.

ALEX OPENED HIS eyes and experienced a blurry white glow. So he shut them and returned to sleep. When he tried again, there were shapes to discern, but not much else, and he noticed a buzzing in his ears. *Gey avek*, fly. Then nothing.

"Who are you?"

When he struggled to see for the third time, there was a person to focus on, but he did not recognize the woman dressed in white. Next, another head hove into view. He smiled at Sarah, but that made his skull hurt.

"Lie still, darling."

Two days later, he sat in bed surrounded by his wife, his sons, and his lieutenants. A cup of water stood on a table and he had been allowed a newspaper that morning.

"We must talk about what happened."

"You must focus all your energy on getting well, Alex."

"Sarah, you are right and wrong in equal measure. There is no point in regaining my strength if some momzer is going to take another crack at me. We need to find them…" He glanced at his sons. "…and neutralize the situation."

"Shall Moishe and I leave the room?"

"I feel it's for the best, David."

Everyone waited for the two children to rejoin their wives and kids in the waiting area.

"Do we know who did it and who issued the contract?"

"The hitman vanished in the dust. It must have been a gun for hire, who returned whence he came."

Alex nodded at Ezra's assessment.

"I am more concerned about who gave the order."

"Our men have rattled every cage in Florida to find a lead, but gornisht."

"Apart from the people in this room, who might want me dead?"

"No need for that, Alex."

"Sarah, I am being honest. I'd understand if Massimo or Ezra took matters into their own hands, given how slow I've been to pass Vegas over to them."

"This wasn't us."

"Massimo, don't be so shamefaced. I am certain it was neither you nor Ezra."

"How can you tell, Alex?"

"Simple, Massimo. I'm still alive. I have enough respect for both of you to know that if you resolve to kill me, you'll get the job done properly."

"Then who?"

"Sarah, it's hard for me to think straight. Whatever drugs they are pushing into my veins are making me groggy."

"Why you and why now?" Ezra glanced at Massimo as he asked this question of Alex. His friend shrugged in response.

"If the order wasn't issued in Florida, it came from somewhere else."

"Right, Massimo. So did one of the Italian families make a move on Alex?"

"Perhaps, but the only business he has left with the mob is Vegas, and Massimo and I are the fronts for that operation. Hitting him wouldn't change any deals set in Nevada."

Alex cleared his throat and took a sip of water. They all turned to listen to his thoughts.

"This wasn't business. It was personal. No one will make any money out of my death, except the recipients of my life policy, and I trust Sarah not to have me whacked."

The couple eyed each other and smiled.

"There are only a handful of people where I know about their criminal pasts and who are still alive. Meyer Lansky, Sam Giancana…"

"You can't believe that Meyer issued the order?"

"No, Sarah. But Sam probably reckons I owe him for Richard Cain. And even if he doesn't, the Feds are breathing down the necks of all the Italian Mafiosi and only a fraction of what I know will send him to the electric chair."

June 1975

33

THE PAIN IN Alex's chest was easing, but all of his body remained a long dull ache with frequent twinges of extreme agony. There were still tubes attached to his arm leading into his nostrils. He had no option but to stay where he was and wait for his torso to heal.

Sarah stayed in Alex's hospital room throughout these days, only leaving to grab a bite to eat and to freshen up. Moishe and David took turns to be by his side, but she bore the brunt of the responsibility. What else was she going to do?

"How long do you figure I'll be stuck in here?"

"The doctors won't say. You're lucky to be alive and they'd rather you continue under observation."

He sighed. That was not what he wanted to hear. It was bad enough that an officer was standing outside the room, but he knew it was a police matter when a bomb went off.

"I'm glad there isn't a Fed guarding me."

"Does it matter, Alex?"

"I trust the Feds less than a local. At least we can bribe a state cop or Miami flatfoot."

"The guy's all right. He leaves us alone and keeps his eyes open."

"That's why I'd rather he wasn't there. He'll include every fella who visits me in his report to his bosses."

"The blast has made you paranoid, Alex."

"If you recall I haven't trusted the Feds for decades. It's not the bomb that makes me paranoid, it's being hounded into prison that did it."

Alex tried to laugh, but it turned into a coughing fit. Each exhalation made his lungs feel like they were going to explode.

"HOW LONG HAVE you been a cop?"

The officer stood next to Alex's bed, legs apart and arms behind his back.

"Three years, sir."

"Do you know who I am?"

"What do you mean, sir?"

"You and your kind have been hunting me all my life and now you guard me. The world's turned upside down."

"All my captain told me is that somebody attacked you and I am here to protect you from any further incident. What you got up to in the past is no concern of mine. Not that I know."

Alex shrugged.

"And what's your name, boy?"

"Patrol Officer Robert O'Neil, sir."

"Did you draw the short straw?"

"Nope. When you first arrived at the hospital, there were three of us here. Two downstairs and another by this room."

"Just following orders, son."

"Not really. I volunteered to be the one who remained."

"Why, Patrol Officer O'Neil?"

"I like to finish things I've started and we haven't caught the culprit yet."

"Noble, Robert."

The patrolman smiled.

"And this is a warm and quiet place to while away a few days."

Now Alex beamed. The boy had a good heart but was lazy. Just perfect.

WHEN HE WOKE up the following day, Sarah was by his side. Her grin filled her face when he opened his eyes.

"How are you doing?"

He coughed and nodded without speaking. Sarah's smile dropped in an instant and she reached out to hold his hand, although he wasn't strong enough to grip her fingers.

"Not too bad. I'll feel better when they pull the tubes out of me."

The oxygen had been positioned in his nose from the moment Sarah had first entered the room on the morning they brought Alex into Jackson Memorial Hospital. He swallowed and tried to move his arm, but the drip prevented him from having much leeway. So he gave up and let his wrist drop back onto the bedcovers.

"I'm worried, Sarah."

"The doctor says you must rest and you should recuperate without any problem. You had a near miss."

"That's not what I meant. I'm concerned that we should deal with Sam Giancana before he makes another move. The greenhorn outside this door won't be effective enough to stop a second attempt on my life."

"There'll be time to handle that matter later. Right now, the important thing is for you to get your strength back. Everything else is toffee."

"We live together. We love together, but we die alone."

"Let everyone look after you and then you can focus on business later on."

He fell silent as he wasn't convinced Sarah was correct, but he couldn't summon the energy to do anything but *shloof*. He closed his eyes to the world and allowed sleep to engulf him.

THAT NIGHT, ALEX lay in bed as the tubes pouring out of his nose continued to annoy him. He'd asked the doctor earlier that day if they could be removed, but the guy said he wanted to continue to monitor his situation overnight before reviewing matters the next day.

All the while, he stared at Patrol Officer Robert O'Neil as he stood guard outside the room. He wished the flatfoot would vamoose, but no luck there. After an hour, his eyelids became heavy and he fell asleep.

In the morning, O'Neil appeared not to have budged an inch, but at least the doctor did his rounds sufficiently early for Alex's liking.

"Well, Mr. Cohen. We can disconnect you from the oxygen today."

"Great news, doc. And when will I be strong enough to get outta here?"

"With your internal injuries, I'd say it'll be a minimum of a week before you are healed adequately for us to let you back into the wild."

"That's way too long. What can we do to speed up the process?"

The doctor smiled.

"I wish we had medicine to increase everybody's recovery rate. You need a simple dose of R & R."

Alex nodded, but there was no reason he should rest in this hospital room a moment longer. While he might not have felt at the top of his game, he had been in far worse states in his life.

ALEX WOKE UP yet again and blinked to get his bearings. He was still at Jackson Memorial and was desperate to leave the joint. There was only one way for this to happen and waiting for the doctor to sign him off was not the fastest route out.

His clothes were hanging in the wardrobe at the other end of his room. Alex swung his legs out of the bed and took a deep breath before he attempted to stand up. As soon as his feet held his weight, he grabbed at the nearby wall to steady himself. This might be harder than he first assumed. Slow and calm.

Ten minutes later and his pants and shirt were hanging on his body. He slumped back onto the mattress and inhaled three times before doing up the buttons on his clothes. He left the bandages on his torso as it would have been more effort to take them off. Every movement was agony, but each step he took made Alex feel a lot better and stronger.

He reached the door and as he turned the knob, O'Neil spun around, his hand on the butt of his gun. The gumshoe would be no barrier for any serious hitman.

"I can't let you out of here, Mr. Cohen."

"Don't take this the wrong way, but it's none of your business. I am leaving this hospital."

"In that case, I must accompany you."

"For my protection?"

"You got it."

"O'Neil, the best chance of me surviving the next few days is if you get the hell out of my path, so that I can take care of this matter myself. If you cops had any idea who was behind the attack, you'd have arrested someone by now. Have you?"

The patrol officer shook his head, eyes cast down at his feet.

"The most I'd like you to do, Robert, is to help me out of the front of the building and call me a cab. After that, you can go back to your station house and tell them I walked away without letting you know where I was going."

"I don't care what you say. I must stay with you."

"Robert, most of the people who do that wind up dead. My life has been a series of hits and the person who stands next to me ends up riddled with bullets, bleeding out on the ground. You got a family?"

"Yes."

"Then I would expect that your wife and kids would like to see you walk through the front door tonight. If that's the case, then you'd better do as I say."

34

THE CAB STOPPED outside Meyer's house, and Alex knocked on the door. Thelma let him in and took him to a sitting room where Meyer was watching television. His friend smiled at him and beckoned to the other end of his couch.

"The game will be over in a short while. Do you mind if I keep it on?"

Alex shrugged and sat down. Baseball held no interest for him, but he knew Meyer enjoyed his sport. The fact he wanted to watch to the final whistle meant he had a six-figure bet on the result. He had stopped believing Meyer's claims to have lost everything in the fall of Havana many years before.

Thelma brought in coffee and cheesecake for both men and then left them alone. Sixty long minutes later, Meyer switched off the television and turned to face Alex.

"So, I hear you've had a spot of bother."

A wince. "Yes, that's about the sum of it."

"How did you shake off the cops? They were stood outside your door in the hospital when I visited."

"I don't remember you coming over."

"It was on the first day and you were still unconscious."

"That makes sense. As for the cop, I pointed out to him that his best interests lay in turning a blind eye."

"Miami's finest strikes again. Does Sarah know you are out of the hospital?"

"No. If she did, she'd send me straight back there, but there's business to attend to."

"By rights, I should call her and put you under the direction of your doctor."

"Meyer, I didn't come here for a lecture. Instead, we must talk about the hit."

"Are you out for revenge?"

"I'm concerned to ensure my family stays safe. If someone must die for me to achieve that security, then so be it."

Meyer nodded and sipped the dregs of his coffee. Then he shuffled out of the room and came back a few minutes later, followed by Thelma and a fresh pot.

"More cheesecake?"

"It tasted wonderful, but I couldn't eat another mouthful, thank you."

"Alex, have you figured out who issued the instruction?"

"Massimo and Ezra scoured the city and found no one, but I reckon I know who ordered my death."

"Who?"

"Surely you have an idea or two on this. What do you reckon?"

"Somebody who wants to alter the power balance in Vegas or an individual with a need to silence you."

"Meyer, I agree. So what names does that imply?"

"Any member of the commission or Sam Giancana?"

"That's what I assumed."

"Have you done anything to rock the boat in Vegas recently?"

"Not that I've noticed. I mean, I still haven't transferred my interests over to Ezra and Massimo. And now I will, although the attack was a very complicated way of making me do what I've been meaning to do for a while."

"That opens the door to your lieutenants organizing the hit, Alex."

"I considered that possibility and discounted it."

"Why?"

"If either of them had done it, then that would destabilize their position at the same time as they held the chips. They'd expect the commission would want to end business with someone who had seized power, rather than demonstrating the patience that natural succession demands. Impatient people are not great to work with and I believe that both Ezra and Massimo are smart enough to appreciate that."

Alex couldn't recall if he'd already had that conversation before with Meyer or somebody else.

"There's another reason it wasn't them, Alex."

"Oh?"

"You are still alive."

"There is that. Sometimes I overthink things, don't I?"

"Now and again, my friend."

"And, Meyer, that's also why I am clear it isn't you."

"Why would I want you dead?"

"Because of what I know."

"Alex, let's just say we possess a shared history and leave it at that."

"My thoughts exactly."

"So where do you stand with Sam Giancana?"

MORE COFFEE, BUT still no more cheesecake. The sun faded outside and Meyer switched on a light. Alex squeezed his eyes shut with the sudden intensity offered by the bulb, but within a couple of minutes, he had grown accustomed to the brightness in the room.

"Do you expect he will try again?"

"Meyer, I would if I were him."

"That wasn't my question though. Will Sam attempt to kill you a second time?"

"If he is attempting to silence me because of what I know of his past, then the fact that the bomb failed to destroy me doesn't change his need to want me dead."

"Why now, Alex?"

"You should understand more than most of us, Meyer. The Feds are breathing down our necks and will seize any opportunity to grab a headline and nail an elderly Mafioso. Higher-ranking individuals than me have ratted out their bosses, so Sam is right not to trust me."

"Has anyone approached you?"

Meyer's eyes narrowed and he stared at Alex. This was no casual question about Alex squealing on Sam. His old friend wanted to know how close he was to spilling his guts about anyone to the cops.

"No, Meyer. I have not."

"Would you tell me if they came to you?"

"Yes, I shall let you know if that ever happens. They've tried to get me to talk before and Dewey got nowhere. Now, I've a better understanding of the jeopardy of refusing to squeal, and I still won't rat out my friends. What's done is done and they can zoygn meyn hon."

"HOW WAS YOUR time leaving Israel, Meyer?"

"Don't get me started. The amount of gelt I gave to that country and they treated me so poorly. Golda Meir, may she rot in hell."

"They made you fly around the world to find a place that would accept you."

"In a sense, Alex. That was more theater on my part. I figured the best way to convince Uncle Sam to let me back in was to make it appear there was nowhere else that would take me."

"Are you telling me you had a choice of where to go and you selected Miami-Dade county?"

"Not quite, but I reckon if I'd had a little more time, then I would have found somewhere in South America to take me, with none of the bull."

"Had you asked Cuba?"

"There's no need to get fresh with me, Alex."

"My apologies, Meyer."

"It took a certain amount of chutzpah to ask Castro for a home, but I felt it might be worth it. Turns out I was wrong."

Alex shook his head in disbelief and muttered, "Only you, Meyer."

"If you don't ask…"

"I know, but Fidel?"

"Alex, I would rather live under that schlemiel than get deported and thrown into jail at my time of life. You, of all people, should understand that."

"I do, Meyer, but still."

His friend's shoulders wobbled up and down and Meyer burst into laughter.

"You thought I'd go cap in hand to that *meeskait*? I assumed you knew me better than that."

Alex returned a blank stare as he processed the information. Then he pointed at his friend and joined in the joke, chuckling at the idea of Meyer living in the ruins of Havana and how easy he had been to dupe.

"You got me good, Meyer."

"Ah, I've been flimflamming people my whole life. You stood no chance."

"WHAT ARE YOU going to do about Giancana, Alex?"

"I don't believe I've much choice."

"In your state? Why not leave it to Ezra, or even Massimo?"

"Because there are some things best done yourself, Meyer."

Thelma popped in and informed them they needed to come to the dinner table where she had prepared some scraps. Alex consumed a few mouthfuls, but he didn't have the energy to eat very much, despite Thelma's protests.

A slice of salt beef and some salad was all he could keep down. Before she could give him a hard time, Meyer reminded her that Alex had left the hospital only a few hours earlier. Then she let him be. Alex and Meyer sat at the table while Thelma cleared away the dregs of their meal.

"What are you going to do?"

"Find the momzer and assassinate him. What else is there? It's him or me."

"After all these years, it has come to this. A Jew must execute an Italian."

"I'm not attacking him because of his ancestry, but due to what he has done and the things he wishes upon me."

"You should pop over to Sarah before you leave."

"Meyer, there is a lot of truth in what you say, but I won't. If I see her, she'll convince me not to go, because she believes my welfare is more important than anything else. That much I've learned since my arrival at Jackson Memorial."

"A man should know he is valued."

"We live together, we love together, but we die alone."

There was only one thing left for Alex to do. He needed to discover where Giancana was located and deal with the fella himself.

"I need to find the whereabouts of a friend of ours."

Massimo grunted on the line.

"We've been trying to locate where he is staying, but nobody has any certain idea."

"Perhaps we could talk about this some more this evening. I'll be on a flight to my second home in a few hours. Can you be there then?"

Alex put down the receiver and thanked Meyer for the use of the phone.

"The least I can do is send a car to take you to the airport."

"You've done enough for me over the years, Meyer. Thank you, but there is no need."

An ordinary cab appeared less than thirty minutes later. Alex hugged his old friend and winced at the pains in his chest. Then the cab whisked him over to the terminal.

35

ALEX TOOK OUT a scrap of paper from his pants pocket. It had fallen out of his newspaper that morning while he was lying in his hospital bed. Although it only contained a name and an address, this was more than he needed to know. He ordered the cab over to Sixth Street and Seventh Avenue, on the cusp of where the Italian and Cuban communities rubbed shoulders.

He was less concerned with reliving the glory of old Havana and preferred to stop the cab around the corner from an apartment block. Inside the building lived Cayson Amato and Alex wanted to have a word with the guy.

Leaning against an alleyway wall over the street from the entrance, he asked himself how many occasions in his life he had spent his hours in a similar situation. He lit a cigarette and contemplated his next move. A quick glance at the names alongside the buzzers in the entranceway indicated Amato was borrowing the place for a while or didn't pay the rent check. No matter, Alex had time on his hands.

Without a description of the guy, most people would have tried pressing every doorbell to find his quarry, but not Alex. Instead, he watched, and he waited. There is something about the way a fella dresses and comports himself that means a knowing eye can recognize you at thirty feet. Sure enough, Alex's patience paid off about an hour after he arrived on the street corner.

A dark-haired boy left the building and strode down the road. His jaw showed he was a man, but his swagger indicated a youthful arrogance that experience had yet to erode. Alex set off to follow him and hoped that an opportunity would arise for him to have a quiet word with the guy.

Cayson stomped toward a corner bodega and Alex waited two doors down. A minute later and Amato reappeared holding a brown bag containing a quart bottle and a pack of cigarettes in his other hand. He stopped for a second only a few paces away from Alex, who concentrated hard on staring into the window display. Once Amato's footsteps receded, Alex turned and followed the plume of smoke back to the apartment block.

"Hey, mac. You got a light?"

Cayson halted on his stoop as Alex showed him a cigarette in need of a flame.

"Sure thing."

The boy remained where he was and let Alex walk up the five steps to reach him. A deep inhalation and he was ready to cup his hands around the spark generated by Cayson's match.

"Thanks."

"Uh-huh."

Amato opened the building door and headed upstairs without looking back. Alex's foot caught the entrance door before it slammed shut and he stood in the lobby, trying to summon the energy to chase Amato up the stairs. Those five steps had taken more out of him than he was expecting.

Perhaps for the first time since he had started smoking, Alex noticed the warmth of the smoke as he inhaled it and the vapors sank into his lungs. He needed to be stronger than this. Just for a short while. He pushed himself up the flight and stopped for a second.

A banging noise above forced Alex to pick up his pace. By the time he reached the third floor, there was only dust in the corridor and a chance to go knocking. "I'm sorry to bother you…" and the woman opposite him slammed the door in his face.

Alex didn't mind as she was not the target of his exercise. The next two people were as welcoming as the first, but the fourth apartment was more intriguing. There was a strong smell of Amato's brand of cigarette by the door. Rat-a-tat-tat.

"You again. What do you want?"

Alex replied by stepping forward half a pace and landing a punch, smack on Cayson's nose, causing him to lose his footing and tumble back.

CAYSON STUMBLED, BUT he didn't fall and grabbed at the walls to regain his balance. He lunged toward the living room and Alex closed the door behind himself. Amato scampered to the open window and the fire escape on the other side, but Alex was too quick and placed a hand on his ankle.

He dragged the boy by his foot, careful to knock Amato's head against any item of furniture nearby, and threw him on the couch. Alex whipped out his revolver and pointed it square at Cayson's temple.

"Don't."

This was the only warning Alex uttered, and the kid relaxed for a second, eyes darting here and there, trying to figure a way out of his situation.

"Is anybody going to appear from any room in this joint?"

"Huh?"

Alex sighed. "Are you alone?" Amato nodded. "If you lie to me, anyone who shows up will get a slug in the belly before I find out it's your mother or a baby. Capeesh?"

"Yes, mister."

"By now, you must wonder what's going on and I shall try to explain. Somebody issued you with a contract to kill me and, as you can tell, you failed to meet your end of the bargain."

"Look, mac—"

"Do not interrupt me, Cayson Amato. Trying to blow me up when my back was turned is one thing, but being rude to my face is quite another."

Alex slapped him on the cheek to get Cayson's attention. The red mark lingered long after.

"Mister, I never…"

"On top of everything else, don't insult me. It was you, Cayson. And use my name."

The boy blinked and inhaled a quick breath.

"Cohen, I was acting under orders."

"Better. Who from?"

"You can't expect me to answer that."

"That's where you are wrong. What you have to understand is that the vow of silence you call omertà only has value if you squeal and remain alive. This will not be a problem for you. The only choice left is whether I kill you slowly or do it quick. Tell me what I want and you'll be gone within a few seconds. Mess me about and we will spend the next day or two in your apartment as you lapse in and out of consciousness with the pain of your situation. And make no mistake, I shall not allow you to die."

Amato's body sank into the couch for a moment as he considered his options. Then he opened his mouth to render his judgment, but instead, he kicked Alex square between the legs and grabbed for the pistol.

Alex curled into a ball with the force of Amato's legwork and as the boy's hands pulled at his fingers, Alex yanked the gun upwards, and the revolver and the palms grappling over its control raced upward and thumped Amato in the jaw. He relaxed his grip for a second, and that gave Alex just enough opportunity to squeeze the trigger.

The slug sailed past Cayson's skull, who ducked left on instinct to avoid the shot. Alex used that moment to rush forward and slammed his head into Amato's torso. On this occasion, the fella slumped down, landing back on the couch. A punch to Alex's stomach and he crumpled again. Only this time, he aimed first before pulling the trigger and a bullet landed in Amato's torso. He tried to pick himself up off the furniture, but Alex got a second bullet into his heart.

Strangely, Alex was the one with a stabbing pain in his lungs and everything faded into black.

ALL ALEX COULD make out was a white ceiling. His chest hurt and his sides ached, but he had no idea where he was or why he was lying on the floor. Then he squeezed his eyes shut and opened them again, and the tussle with Amato flooded back into his mind.

He flailed his arms around as he tried to sit up. There was a sticky dampness on his left hand: blood. Alex checked himself and exhaled in relief as he was all right. A glance at the couch told a different story for Cayson Amato, whose body was awash with red. The night sky was visible from Alex's vantage point; he must have been out of it for several hours.

Another blink and Alex staggered to his feet, holding onto a nearby chair until he felt steady enough to wander off to the kitchen to grab a mouthful of water from the faucet. He couldn't tell whether to throw up or sort out the mess next door. He spat out a second gulp of liquid and lit a cigarette.

When he returned to the living room, Alex saw his fingerprints were all over the bloody river emanating from Amato's corpse. There was enough evidence on those floorboards to send him away for the rest of his life. He searched the apartment for a mop and bucket.

When none was forthcoming, he did the next best thing, removed a shirt from Cayson's wardrobe, and soaked up the liquid from the floor around the fella's body. Unless he planned on dumping the corpse somewhere else, this was all he was prepared to do.

Alex checked each room for any sign of his existence. The only item was the butt of his cigarette, which he threw into the sink and washed down the plughole. Then he put his ear to the door and listened out for Amato's neighbors.

Voices. He held his breath with a hand on the handle and the other holding his gun. Whoever it was, the talking faded away, and a door closed farther down the corridor. Alex waited for a count of one hundred before opening the door a crack and poking his head out.

Nothing. He scurried down the stairs, but when he reached the lobby, he had to stop to catch his breath again. With no shadows to hide in, Alex's heart was rattling away at a thousand beats a minute. *Deep breaths*. When he felt he could move, Alex exited the building and hightailed it along the street, turned left at the corner, and strode four blocks at a normal pace.

Then he stood with his arm outstretched until a cab pulled over.

"Take me to the airport."

36

HE STOOD IN a long line to buy a one-way ticket to Palm Springs. By the time the transaction was complete, Alex headed to the nearest seating to have a rest. His heart thumped inside his chest cavity and his stomach couldn't decide whether to ache or cramp. When he regained his breath, he hobbled over to a pharmacy concession and picked up some painkillers. Then he knocked back three pills over a cup of coffee in the lounge.

As he took a sip to enjoy the flavor of his drink, he glanced over to the other end of the waiting area. He blinked and stared again. Was that Gerry Droller? Alex stood up and walked toward the guy, but by the time he reached the other side of the room, the guy had moved away.

Alex hadn't seen the man since the Bay of Pigs. Or rather, that was the last time he had looked at Droller for sure. When he stood behind Sirhan Sirhan and whacked Bobby Kennedy, Alex believed he'd spotted Droller in the corridor, but he hadn't the opportunity nor the inclination to stop and check. After all, he'd just assassinated the politician most people thought was going to become the next President of the United States of America.

He shrugged and returned to his seat, but he felt the flutter in his aching stomach as the adrenaline rushed through his veins. What was Droller doing in Miami at the same time as he was traveling to Palm Springs? More important than that, what if it wasn't a coincidence? The last thing he needed was to be hounded by the CIA.

Before Alex could ponder the problem any further, the public address system announced the departure of his flight. He stood up and waited for his fellow passengers to make their way through the lounge and out to the gate. As they threaded between chairs and concessions, he peered as far forward as he could, hoping to see Droller again.

By the time he reached the airstairs, Droller had vanished from sight. So he was either a figment of Alex's imagination or was waiting inside. Whichever was the case, Alex knew he must get on the jet and head toward his destiny.

ONCE THE PLANE was in the air, Alex walked along its length to see if he could spot Droller, but no matter how much he stared at the strangers before him, the guy was nowhere to be found. Alex sauntered back to his seat and winced as he sat down. The stabbing aches in his side were not abating and he popped another mouthful of painkillers.

He woke up with a jolt when the wheels hit the ground and shook his head to fling the last vestige of sleep from his mind. As he had picked a window seat, Alex let every other passenger file past before he exited the plane. If he had missed Droller, then the guy was in front of him and would find it much harder to follow Alex out of the airport.

As he waited in line for a cab, Alex's head darted left and right as he stayed vigilant, in case Droller doubled back on him in the terminal. Nothing. He tried to relax, but a nagging doubt remained in the pit of his stomach. Alex knew what he had seen and the fact the man vanished did not change matters at all.

For a second, he caught his breath as he recalled the landing in the Bay of Pigs and the taste of sand in his mouth. Then he flitted to kissing the earth in those French trenches decades before.

A prod on his shoulder and Alex blinked. The man behind him in the line was tired of waiting.

"You getting into a cab, mac?"

Alex nodded by way of apology and hopped into the yellow vehicle. In less than a minute, the cab left the grounds of the airport and was hurtling to the city center.

WITH THE IMAGE of Droller still filling his head, Alex chose not to go direct to his second house, but to split his journey into two legs. The cab pulled up outside the Palm Springs Country Club and Alex tipped the driver.

Despite talking about it frequently, Alex had tinkered with golf, but now in the clubhouse, he was surrounded by men who cared about the sport more than Alex judged possible for a single human being.

He asked for an outside table so he could soak in the sun for a little while and ordered his usual breakfast, although he did not know what time it was. The bagel took some chewing, but he swallowed it all, though his Herculean effort was only achieved by using up all his orange juice. He caught a waitress's eye and pointed at his now-empty glass.

He nibbled at his fruit salad, but couldn't face even a bite of a cheese blintz. Still, Alex remained where he sat for over an hour, watching golf balls land near the eighteenth hole. But most of his time was spent looking inside the restaurant and not out at the rolling green lawns.

If Droller had followed him here, the guy would need to show himself eventually. There was no vantage point from the fairway, so that meant if the fella was in the vicinity, then he'd have to sit at a table or hover in the background. A scout round on a trip to the bathroom showed Alex that the ex-CIA operative was nowhere to be found.

Alex returned to his seat and called for the check. Once he paid it, he wandered to the front reception and asked for someone to call him a cab.

"Where to, sir?"

"The airport."

The lie was Alex's last effort to shake Droller from his tail. But a short wait later and another yellow cab hurtled around the streets of Palm Springs. This time, it screeched to a halt outside his house.

37

EZRA AND MASSIMO had already arrived and were waiting for him in the kitchen.

"Want some coffee?"

"I'm glad you've made yourself at home, Massimo."

The Italian smiled and waited to find out if he needed to pour another mug. The drink scalded the roof of Alex's mouth, but it tasted good when the feeling returned to his palate. He wandered off to the veranda as the sun was out and he wanted to enjoy the warmth on his skin.

After a few minutes' hunt in an outhouse building, Ezra found cushions for the patio furniture and they settled down to hear what Alex required of them.

"I need to speak to the commission."

Massimo's eyebrows shot to the top of his forehead and Ezra's jaw dropped an inch.

"No disrespect, Alex, but do you expect that's even possible?"

"I see no reason why they should refuse."

"Giancana said the commission had decreed you must never be seen by any of them. It's pretty clear cut to me."

"Ezra, that decision was made when the bosses only wanted a quiet life and no more. From what I've read, the bombing hit the pages of the national press. That is not the sort of publicity the commission wants."

"Times have changed, all right."

Alex nodded at Massimo.

"I have always said that we live together, we love together. It's time Sam Giancana died alone."

"And you want the commission to authorize the hit?"

"I wouldn't go rogue at my age, now would I?"

"HOW WILL WE get you in front of the most powerful men in the country?"

"The answer is simple. You shall use your Italian contacts to arrange a meeting."

Massimo's cheeks lost their color and he took a large swig of his coffee. The corner of Ezra's mouth curled a little. Alex turned his head to speak to his other lieutenant.

"And you will facilitate safe passage when everything is agreed, Ezra."

"Do you need us to operate as intermediaries?"

"Ezra, you both understand that nobody close to the commission will even take my call. So somebody must act as a go-between. Who else could I trust more with this task? It's the last thing I shall ever ask of you."

"Don't talk like that, Alex."

"No, I mean there will be no more favors or accommodations from me once you help me get to the commission. Today, at this table, I pass on all my Vegas interests to you both in an equal share, without condition or consideration."

"We must give you something for it."

"If you want to donate to my family's business, I will not refuse such a gesture. But I am not asking you for a single cent."

"You're a generous fella, Alex Cohen."

"And you are going to place a call to whoever you know with access to the commission's ear and arrange a meeting, Massimo."

THE ITALIAN RETURNED to the patio twenty minutes later. The man played poker well and Alex could not read anything into his expression at all.

"How'd you get on?"

"One step forward and two steps back."

"What do you mean, Massimo?"

"No matter how hard I argued, there is no way on this planet I can find someone to bring you in front of the commission."

Alex opened his mouth and his lieutenant raised a hand to stop him in his tracks.

"That's the bad news. The good news is that a member of the commission will receive you. If you can reach an accommodation with him, it is all you need. No member of the commission itself will risk meeting in one place just because you want their cooperation."

"After all these years, Appalachia still hangs above their heads."

Massimo nodded and sighed.

"It was the best I could do."

"You have done well. Thank you, my friend."

"One of us should go with you."

"And why is that, Ezra?"

"To help keep you safe."

"If the commission had sanctioned the hit, someone would have paid me a visit in the hospital and finished the job. And as it wasn't them, I must assume they bear me no ill will."

"You are putting your life on the line all by yourself, Alex, when the only thing we are suggesting is that somebody watches your back."

"If Giancana has gunned for me once, he will try again. Not today, maybe not tomorrow, but at some point, and who knows what will take place then? Sarah could have been in the car with me. My children or the grandkids might be next to me when a stray bullet lands. I can't permit that to happen. I shall stop this matter in its tracks and nobody else must be put in harm's way. So I thank you for your kind offer, but I will do this alone."

Ezra shook his head and Massimo sipped his coffee. In response, Alex lit a cigarette and waited.

"Have you considered the possibility that this might be a trap? That Giancana was executing the hit on the commission's say-so?"

"If you are right, I will head to certain death. But if I do nothing, Giancana will redouble his efforts, I will be dead, and I'll have put my family in the firing line."

"I asked for the talk to take place in a public area, a cafe or restaurant. That way, you know they won't whack you in the meeting itself."

"Thanks, Massimo, but it makes no difference."

"It does to me, Alex. The least I can do is make sure you are as safe as possible."

"You are both good men. I must admit at one point, I wondered if you'd put the contract out."

The two lieutenants smiled. Ezra was the first to break the embarrassed silence.

"Don't think we didn't consider it a few years ago. We were angry with you for a while until we realized you just didn't want to let go, not because you didn't trust us."

"I believed I was clear in expressing my thoughts to you, but I should have explained things better. It was all about me and never about you. Sorry."

The men shuffled, uncertain how to respond to Alex's admission, so they chose silence and sips of coffee.

"Will you keep this place on, now that you don't need to be so close to Vegas?"

"I haven't thought about it, Ezra. I guess it's nice to have a second home farther north."

"If you decide to sell, let me know and I shall offer you a good price."

"Thanks, I'll bear it in mind."

38

"HOW ARE YOU doing?"

"I was worried, Alex. Why did you leave the hospital without telling me?"

"I figured you'd try to stop me and there's some business I need to take of, Sarah."

"What you must do is look after yourself."

"Believe me, I've not been running around painting the town red. I don't have the energy."

"Come home, Alex."

"I will soon, but not just yet."

"I won't waste my breath asking you where you are, because I know you won't say. But tell me you will not do anything dumb."

"Just smart moves from me for the foreseeable future, Sarah."

"Now you are mocking me. I thought you might have been kidnapped."

"No one would be that stupid. Everybody understands you'd refuse to pay the ransom."

"That's not funny, Alex."

"I know, but I thought I'd tease you anyway."

"How long before I should expect you home?"

"It's going to take a few days, maybe a week."

"How are you holding up?"

"Not too bad. I've got some meds from the hospital that help keep me ticking over. Apart from the occasional twinge, I'm fine."

"I miss you."

"Straight back at you."

ANOTHER PLANE, ONLY this time it touched down in LaGuardia. Alex had the sense to spend the night in Palm Springs before flying across the country. Despite the bravado he had shown Sarah, he knew he was not in good shape. The pains in his chest and side were getting worse and there was only so much that his painkillers could do. But he had no choice.

He sent his cab to Little Italy and got out at the top of Mulberry. From there, he zigzagged all over the neighborhood until he arrived at a family-run restaurant off the main drag. He glanced around the tables until he spotted a customer he recognized.

"Thank you for meeting me, Joe."

"You're welcome, Alex."

Joe Batters was one of the few commission members that Alex still knew on a personal level. They might not have seen each other for a few years, or spoken to each other for even longer, but they remembered a world before so many bosses lost a bundle in Havana. Joe had controlled Chicago in his vicelike grip until he passed the mantle over to Giancana, but the fella didn't retire. Instead, he became consigliere and weathered the storm of Sam's high-profile lifestyle.

The men ordered a bowl of pasta each and maintained a level of small talk until the waiter had the good sense to leave them alone.

"I appreciate you agreeing to meet with me, Joe."

"After what happened to you, how could I refuse?"

"My understanding is that there are many in the commission who will not forgive me for some of my past indiscretions."

"Alex, I cannot speak for others, but I am not aware of any ill will from any of my business associates."

He paused for a second and soaked in the information that Giancana had lied to him.

"I was led to believe that, after '68, I was not welcome at any Italian meetings."

Joe put down his silverware and ran his tongue around his teeth. After a sip of red wine, he placed another forkful of linguini to his lips.

"The matter came up in conversation, but there was no malice toward you. If the rumors of your involvement were correct, then there was gratitude for helping to remove an unwanted pest from our business dealings."

"Do you know why Sam Giancana told me otherwise?"

"He was not authorized to do so by the commission, Alex."

"Sam stated that there had been a vote and that I was no longer to attend any meetings involving Italian businessmen."

"That explains why you vanished from the world."

Alex nodded and reflected on those wasted years when he could have been building an empire.

"What's done is done, Joe. I wish us to talk about more recent events."

"Go on."

"Giancana instigated the hit on me and I seek permission to resolve the matter."

"What do you intend to do?"

"My family is at risk while I am being hunted and I would like the commission to offer them protection."

"Alex, let me get this straight. You want to pay protection to us for your wife and children?"

"And the entire extended family. I need to be certain that everybody I love is safe. Even after I'm gone."

"Do you have a sum in mind?"

"Joe, I wasn't thinking of paying any money at all. We both realize that Giancana has returned to America and might well end up in front of a grand jury. None of our friends wish that to happen. So, in exchange for my family's security, I offer to resolve the question of Sam Giancana."

"You expect the commission to approve a hit on a former boss and commission member?"

"Joe, as you ask me so bluntly, then yes. The *farmishte pisk* must die."

They fell silent and chewed through the rest of their food. Alex glanced up at Joe once or twice but did his best to give the man time to ponder. Perhaps he should have listened to Ezra and brought some backup.

Another sip of wine.

"Misrepresenting my business partners is a serious matter, but not enough to warrant the response you propose. However, given your control of Las Vegas, the bombing of your car should have been approved at a higher level. For that, Giancana must pay. I will permit the hit, but I insist on having one of my men accompany you."

"I operate on my own."

"Alex, if we are to whack this man, then I shall have a witness at the scene to confirm the act has been completed, and that it is done with respect."

39

JOE INVITED ALEX to stay overnight in a comped suite at the Waldorf-Astoria Hotel. That way, he would be comfortable, but there would be no record of his being in New York; Alex always paid cash for his flights and used a false driving license so that his name was never on any airplane manifest.

As he sank into his mattress, Alex's mind wandered to Arnold Rothstein's New Year parties in the ballroom down below. Different times. To snap himself out of his reverie, he phoned Sarah and enjoyed the warmth of her voice.

"Will you be back soon?"

"The timing hasn't changed since yesterday, but things are moving on quicker than I anticipated they would. The matter will get resolved in the next few days."

"Do you still have your meds?"

"Enough to keep me going. I might ask my host to source some more."

THE PHONE ON his nightstand rang and Alex woke and bolted upright in a second. He grabbed the receiver.

"Hello?"

"I'm downstairs. Are you ready to meet me in the lobby or must I come up?"

"It'll take me twenty minutes to freshen up and then I want some breakfast. You choose."

"Expect a knock in a minute."

Sure enough, in the time it took Alex to find a dressing gown, there was a thump on the door and he greeted Anthony Spilotro.

"Make yourself comfortable while I get ready."

"That's the plan, Cohen."

"Call me Alex."

"Hurry and quit your jabbering."

With that instruction ringing in his ears, Alex sauntered to the bedroom and took his sweet time getting ready. Spilotro wasn't a people person, but then his role had nothing to do with keeping Giancana happy.

Room service arrived just as Alex finished putting on his clothes and he sat in the living area to eat his breakfast: one bagel, orange juice, a cheese blintz, and coffee.

"Want some?"

Alex waved the pot in Spilotro's general direction, who nodded but did not stand up. Alex placed the mug on the table. "Here it is if you want it." A heavy sigh and Spilotro hauled ass and collected his drink. Then he slumped into a chair opposite Alex.

"You understand that the earlier we start, the sooner we can both get back to our lives."

"Anthony, what you must know is that this is my life. There is nothing else I wish to do other than to terminate Sam Giancana. The only rush on my part is that his death will mean my family is safe. So, call Joe and tell him I need some more meds."

Alex threw the bottle at Spilotro, who caught it through sheer instinct. A grunt and he headed to the phone. Some brief conversation took place, and he hung up.

"They'll be over in thirty minutes."

"Thank you, Anthony."

"When Joe asked me to watch over you, he didn't mention how high in his regard you must be."

"What do you mean?"

"When we pay somebody to whack a fella, we don't cover subsistence requests."

"Anthony, the situation is more complicated than you might imagine. No money is changing hands and, before you ask, this is no favor I am performing for Joe. We go back a long time."

"All the way to Chicago?"

"And some. Suffice to say we both knew Alfonse Capone."

"My respect, Alex."

"He's dead and we are alive. Let's work together to keep it that way."

THE NEXT STEP after Alex's medicine arrived was to head out to Queens. Spilotro stopped their driver outside a residential block. They left the limo and were buzzed in.

"Let me do all the talking, Alex. Idrissa can be tetchy with strangers."

"Whatever works best, Anthony."

Much to Alex's relief, they took the elevator to the fifth floor and Spilotro led them down the corridor until they reached door 5G. Rat-a-tat-tat and Idrissa appeared after a few seconds. He glanced left and right, and then walked back inside, muttering as the men followed him through the hallway.

When Idrissa stopped, Alex glanced around the room. There was a kitchenette on the right-hand side and two doors, one open and the other closed. A bed was visible, so he guessed the bathroom was shut off from plain sight.

"How are you doing, my man?"

"Just fine. As pleasant as it is for you folks to visit me, I've got places to go, so if we could get business conducted sharpish, I'd be much obliged."

"No worries, Idrissa. My friend and I can leave conversation for the next occasion."

The guy eyed Alex from head to toe and sucked on his teeth.

"There won't be another time with this dude, Anthony. I don't like the way he stares at people."

Alex shrugged and averted his gaze. He had no desire to start anything with their gun dealer, who nodded at Anthony and vanished into the bedroom for a minute. When he returned, he carried a suitcase, which he dropped onto a coffee table and opened up to reveal a host of firearms.

Everyone sat down and Idrissa took out a few choice items. Anthony felt the weight of three of the revolvers and passed two over to Alex to try. The .22 seemed passable, and he noted how both the trigger and butt were taped up. No fingerprints were going to linger on these babies. Anthony selected a .44 for himself, which Alex had found too heavy.

"How much for the pair?"

"Fifty each and ten for three boxes of ammo."

"Your prices have gone up, Idrissa."

"From what I hear, you're more important now, which makes me guess you are getting a bigger paycheck. You know you can afford it, and my product is untraceable."

"Call it a round hundred and you got yourself a deal."

Idrissa considered for a second and held out his hand to shake. Spilotro took it and smiled. Then he pulled out a pistol from his pocket and shot the dealer in the face. Alex stood up and tried to escape the spray of blood pouring out of the guy's eyeball.

"If you'd told me that was your plan, Anthony, I wouldn't have got so close."

"The mook was getting greedy. Let's grab the pieces and slugs and get out of here."

They pulled all the boxes of ammo out of the case that they needed and Anthony rummaged through Idrissa's pants pocket and removed a roll of greenbacks. He offered some to Alex, who refused.

"You can pay for dinner tonight instead."

His partner was satisfied with that suggestion and they exited the apartment block, into the waiting limo, and away.

THEY ATE IN Little Italy that evening; Alex had a steak and fries, choosing not to break the habit of a lifetime.

"Have you got any other surprises up your sleeve, Anthony?"

"What do you mean?"

"The situation with Idrissa. I wouldn't have objected if you told me beforehand that you were going to whack him. That would have been your business."

"Alex, to be honest, I didn't know it would happen until we shook hands. The sweat on his palm made me wonder how many more times we'd work together before something went south with the deal. And I wasn't prepared to wait and find out."

"Anthony, we all do what we must, but if you and I are going to embark on a trip to Chicago, I want to know that you will keep a level head when we arrive there. We do not need any surprises."

"I have been on countless hits before and they have all been peachy. Don't fret so much."

"Anthony, I like to think through all the angles as part of my preparation for a job. That way, I am less likely to be caught unawares during its execution. It is not worry, but an attempt to be ready for any eventuality which might occur when we are in the field."

"Call it whatever you like, Alex. There's no point in fussing. We will go in, bam, and out again. No fuss, no bother."

"I admire your optimism, but nothing ever goes that smoothly in my experience."

"You haven't been a Spilotro sidekick until now."

Alex chose not to respond. Anthony's reputation was well known as an effective mob associate, and there was no need to be concerned that he wouldn't be able to handle his end of the situation. It was the way he appeared to behave that gave Alex cause for concern.

He was not comfortable with the fella's casual approach to planning. And the speed with which Spilotro decided to kill Idrissa meant Alex could not be sure he'd walk out of Giancana's house alive, or if he would ever see Sarah again.

40

OAK PARK WAS just one of the many suburbs of Chicago and appeared to be the same as the outskirts of any other American city. There were picket fences and local stores, kids on bikes, and parents with strollers. As their limo crawled around the streets in Giancana's neighborhood, Alex felt like he knew this place, even though he had never been there before.

"Does this vehicle stand out in this part of town?"

"Not at all, Alex. I've visited Sam several times since he got back to the States from his Mexican vacation."

The answer satisfied him and as they drove by the front of Giancana's house, he wondered how they were going to get inside. Although he had no way of knowing it, Anthony explained that the dude with the bulge in his jacket pocket standing outside Sam's porch was a plainclothes cop.

"You mean Giancana is about to testify?"

"Yeah, there's an investigation into the mob and the CIA. Can you believe that? The goombah is going to spill his guts about what he did with Lee Harvey Oswald."

Alex swallowed hard. That explained why Joe was so quick to agree to a Giancana hit; someone had to do it, and he had volunteered like a *schlemiel*. What a fool he had been. An extra day's wait in hospital and Anthony would have been dispatched to do the deed and he'd have stayed where he was.

Now that he was in the middle of all this, the least he should do was to ensure he didn't let Anthony finish the fella off. It sounded like they were far too tight. Sam Giancana must die.

"WE COULD WAIT until it's dark and take a rifle shot from the front. That way, the cop on the stoop can stay where he is and we needn't worry about him."

"Anthony, I suppose the sniper is me and this is your way of saying that somehow I do not have to be concerned about poking a barrel out of our limo window and aiming past the head of local law enforcement."

Spilotro smiled and shrugged, then took an enormous bite out of his pastrami sandwich. They had traveled a mile away to sit down in a deli and stretch their legs. The saloon was comfortable but was not designed for two men, plus a driver, to remain inside it for several hours staring at a house. There was no washroom for a start.

Alex nibbled on a bagel but wasn't really hungry. His chest continued to annoy him, and he used his pills to take the gnawing ache away. A slug of coffee washed the cobwebs out of his head, and he focused on the problem at hand.

"If we can't come up with anything better, then you can buy a rifle and I'll do it, but you understand that there is a strong chance Sam'll survive and the cop will meet his maker."

"There's one in the trunk. We always pack for every occasion."

"So why did we bother with Idrissa?"

"I wanted to find out what you'd do under pressure, Alex."

"You verstinkener momzer."

Spilotro's expression darkened and Alex realized he had hurt the big lunk's feelings. If Anthony had been one of his people, then he'd have given him a quick slap to put him in his place. But he would never have had Spilotro in his crew anyway.

AS ANTHONY WAS a known figure in Oak Park, he was less bothered about being seen on the streets than Alex. After another four hours in the back of the car, he relented, and they walked around for a while, although Alex was careful to keep the brim of his fedora over his eyes.

Each of the houses on Giancana's road were the same. Two stories with a basement and a double garage on the first floor. There was a set of steps leading up to the first-floor front door and a cellar was visible from the street, although it had no separate entrance. Anyone entering the premises from the front would be seen by every neighbor who looked out of their window, as well as by the cop who remained at his post on the stoop throughout his shift.

"If one of us distracted the flatfoot, do you imagine the other might slip in behind him?"

"Anthony, these guys wear a dumb uniform, but they aren't that stupid. There must be a better way than that. What if we made a bigger distraction? One that would draw the sentry not just away from the house, but away from the street altogether."

"What are you thinking of, Alex?"

"If there was a major incident, then the cop would have to assist. Even if he was on foot, right?"

"I suppose. Anything particular you got in mind?"

"A robbery? A car chase? Report of bullets fired around the corner?"

"That's not bad. We walk up the steps, ring the bell and when Giancana appears, then we let rip with all guns blazing."

"Not quite what I was imagining, Anthony."

A DINER FOR their evening meal and Alex chose the steak and fries, although he didn't finish his dinner and hid the last quarter of the meat under his silverware.

"Looks like we should find a place to sleep for the night. This problem will not get solved in the next hour; we've been circling round it the whole day."

"We sure need to have some rest, but I reckon we are closer than you might imagine."

"How so?"

"Anthony, have we seen Giancana even from a window?"

"No, not once."

"So, how do we know that he's inside at all?"

"You mean we don't?"

"Not quite. If Sam wasn't holed up in that house, then the cop would have moved on to something more important. And that means that Giancana is indoors, but he's making certain not to be visible from the outside."

"No sniper shot then, Alex."

"Nope. Not on this occasion."

Anthony ordered another coffee, but Alex wasn't in the mood for one himself.

"I believe it's time we tested out our sentry. Until now, we have been giving him a wide berth and we need to determine what he's made of."

ALEX STROLLED DOWN along Fillmore Street toward the corner with South Wenonah, where Sam's house was located. Hands in his pockets, he walked up to the flatfoot who stood on the stoop. The cop hadn't moved more than three feet from earlier. He sure was a dedicated member of law enforcement.

"Excuse me, officer, but I'm lost. Can you give me some directions?"

The guy nodded and hopped down the five steps to reach Alex.

"Where are you trying to get to?"

"That's my problem. I'm meeting a friend of mine in a bar and he said it was on Fillmore, but here I am and there's nowhere to drink that I've found. Any idea where he might have meant?"

The cop eyed him up and down and rested his chin in his hand.

"You're correct. There's no drinking establishment anywhere near. You sure you heard your buddy correctly?"

"There was a lot of background noise, so maybe I got it wrong. You know of any bar near these parts at all?"

"No, sir. This is all residential around here. Your best plan would be to call your friend back and get some more details from him."

"Thanks. Where is the nearest pay phone, please?"

"That I do know." He pointed in the direction from which Alex had come. "Two blocks that way to Maple Park, left one block and you'll find a kiosk on the corner."

"Mighty obliged, officer."

When Alex reached the limo, he popped inside and relayed the news to Anthony.

"The cop is just a kid. There was mud on his shoes and his top button was loose. Also, he left his station for a minute to help me, so it is a reasonable assumption that if we create a diversion, then he will leave his post again."

"Only this time, we'll take him far away from the real action."

THEY SLEPT IN a fleapit on the other side of town and ate breakfast in a diner along the street. Alex only wanted a bagel, which he washed down with orange juice. Then he asked for a coffee.

"Looks like we've got the makings of a plan, Anthony. Speak to your people today and agree on a time for shots to be fired two blocks away."

"We don't need to bother anyone else. We can trust Michael to miss, be as loud as possible, and not get caught."

"Michael?"

"Our driver. You've been stuck inside a tin can with him for how long and you didn't figure out his name by now?"

"I have a lot on my mind."

Anthony snorted and slurped his coffee.

"When that boy in a man's uniform goes to investigate the mystery gunfire, we'll enter from the backyard and do for Sam Giancana."

41

THE THREE MEN stepped out of the limo, and Michael walked round the back to pop the trunk. Anthony bent over and produced a baseball bat, which he tried to hide beneath his coat.

"What are you doing with that thing?"

"It never hurts to come prepared, Alex."

"We're not hopping over to play ball with the fella. This is man's work; only boys mess around with bats."

Anthony threw the stick back into the trunk and shrugged. Michael closed the hood and checked his piece.

"Are we all set? Michael, give us a short while to get to the backyard and then fire into the sky by Maple Park."

"I got it, Alex. As soon as I let rip, I'll hightail it back here and wait for you guys to surface."

"Good. If you have to stick around more than thirty minutes, then drive off and forget you ever knew us."

"Not quite, Alex. If we take that long, then Michael informs Joe Batters what happened, but nobody else. You understand?"

Michael nodded at Anthony and set off in the opposite direction from the two other men.

ANTHONY LED ALEX to the corner of Harvard Street and South Winonah Avenue, one block north of Giancana's home.

"There is no direct route to the rear of his house. We have to clamber our way south between the back of the houses, with Winonah on our left and Wisconsin Avenue on our right."

When they'd scampered the length of the block, Alex asked to stop for a minute to regain his breath. Before them stood Giancana's backyard, with no access from the front, just as Spilotro had described. There was a lawn and a patio area, along with three doors. One was on the far right and Alex reckoned that headed to the garage, based on the time he had spent staring at the frontage over the last day.

One of the other entrances was on the same level as the grass, while the other led down to the basement, which had the only lights on in the building. No prizes for guessing where Sam was ensconced.

They hunkered down at the back of the lawn, hidden by the leaves of a small tree, positioned next to a shed.

"Now we wait."

Three minutes later and Michael's revolver let rip so the entire neighborhood could hear. Alex counted to sixty, and then the two men scurried across the yard. Anthony tried the handle of the first-floor door and it opened with no fuss. Alex pulled out his .22, and they entered the home of Sam Giancana.

THE DOOR TOOK them straight into a living room, which would have enjoyed a pretty view of the backyard during daylight hours. Anthony led Alex through the house; after all, he knew his way around well enough. Into a corridor with a flight of stairs leading upward and a separate set heading to the basement. The glow of light from below helped Alex join the dots.

Anthony padded downstairs first, and Alex followed. When both arrived at the foot of the stairs, they found the silhouette of a fella sitting at a kitchen table reading a newspaper. He raised his head for a second and continued to peruse the paper.

"Don't skulk. If you're in this room, then at least have the decency to walk up to me like a man."

Anthony stepped forward and Alex waited in the shadows, gun pointing straight at Giancana's back.

"Hi, Sam. I figured I'd pay you a visit as I haven't been around for a while."

"Good to see you, Anthony. Are you going to introduce me to your friend, or is he intending to hide for the evening?"

Alex walked into the light, and Sam nodded at him.

"It's been a long time, Alex."

Sam's eyes fixed on Alex's pistol for a moment and then he turned his attention back to Anthony.

"How's the outside world?"

"Same old, Sam. There's always some business that needs sorting out."

"How was Mexico?"

Giancana smiled.

"Pleasant mostly, but I figured I had been abroad long enough. So here I am."

Alex took another couple of paces toward Sam and put his gun away. Anthony removed his empty hand from his pants pocket.

"Sit down, the pair of you and I'll cook us something to eat."

"I'm not hungry, thank you."

"If you say so, Alex. Anthony, will you join me in some sausages and peppers?"

"How can I refuse, Sam?"

The fella stood up and walked over to a larder. Alex removed his focus from Giancana and noticed the basement had been converted into a summer kitchen, complete with a dining table and chairs, as well as a cooking area with a fridge and sink. Sam grabbed some bell peppers from a shelf and chopped them into small pieces. Then he opened the refrigerator to reveal a bowl containing sausages. He took a handful and sliced them too.

THE TWO MEN stared at Giancana as he set about pouring some olive oil into a frying pan and turning up the heat until it sizzled. He threw in the peppers first, followed by the sausage a minute later. All the while, he stirred.

"My mama used to cook this, but kids today expect it to be made with tomato sauce and served with pasta."

Sam shook his head, and Anthony glanced in Alex's direction and shrugged.

"Do me a favor, Anthony, and grab some forks from that drawer."

The man did as he was bid and dropped the silverware on the table. Sam smiled, but Alex frowned. If he didn't know better, he would have been certain that Giancana knew their plan and was doing his level best to derail them.

"Sam, why don't you put the spoon down and sit at the table?"

"But why?"

Giancana's eyes traveled from his frying pan to Alex's face, and back to his cooking.

"It's ready, anyway. Sure you don't want some, Alex?"

Alex shook his head and Sam poured the contents of the pan into two bowls and brought them to the table.

"Come. Sit."

Anthony followed Giancana's instructions and sat opposite the former mob boss, but Alex moved to stand at the head of the table.

"You understand that this isn't only a social visit, Sam?"

"I figured something like that."

Alex tilted his head to one side.

"There's a rumor you are about to squeal to the Feds. That's why they've put a guard on your front door."

Sam peered out of the front window, but there was only a streetlight to be seen. If there was a cop on the stoop, there was no way to spot him from here in the basement.

"I ain't no rat."

"That is what I assumed, Sam. It's what I told Anthony. We live together, we love together…"

"But we die alone. I remember what you always said, Alex. And as there are three of us in this room, then I know I am safe. Do you expect I will spill my guts to a stranger?"

"I dunno, Sam. Are you?"

"Alex, you two should get your story straight, because Anthony here sounds like he doesn't believe me either."

"Sam, you need to understand that I am not here because I believe you will break your vow of omertà. That's between you and the commission."

Sam continued to eat his sausage and peppers, blowing on each forkful before popping it in his mouth and chewing. Anthony's hands had returned to his pants pockets.

"You're not touching your food, Anthony."

"I'm not hungry after all, Sam."

"It happens."

Giancana carried on, plowing his home-cooked meal past his lips, speeding up until he began to cough. Yet still more kept being shoveled in. He coughed again, and then he put a hand to his esophagus and started retching. Anthony stood up alongside Giancana, who clung to the edge of the table and indicated for Anthony to slap him on the back.

In that instant, Giancana swiveled around and came round Anthony's back, placing a knife at his throat. Alex whipped out his pistol and aimed it at Giancana's head.

"Uh-uh, Alex. I'll slit him from ear to ear before any bullet you fire reaches me."

Giancana fumbled in Anthony's pockets and pulled out his revolver, and threw it on the floor, away from all of them.

"Sam, I hope you aren't making the mistake of believing I care whether Anthony lives or dies. This isn't about him, and I told you before, this is not about what you are going to tell the authorities about anything to do with the Kennedys."

"I ain't no rat."

"It doesn't matter, Sam. This is about you and me."

"What do you mean?"

"The car bomb, Sam: it was you."

"You have me mixed up with some other fella."

"Don't be ridiculous, Sam." Giancana clenched the knife tighter in his palm and pressed the blade closer to Anthony's throat. "I know you ordered the hit on me."

"I just said it wasn't me. You've got your wires crossed."

Alex blinked—he had worked it all out. Sam authorized the contract without the commission's permission. Joe told him that. Besides, there was nobody else on the planet who might want him dead. He lowered his gun hand by an inch.

Sam pushed Anthony forward, so the lunk headed straight at Alex, while the old boss rushed for the stairs. Alex sidestepped the Italian, who regained his balance before he crashed into the stove behind Alex. Giancana's foot reached the first step. Alex straightened his shooting arm and squeezed the trigger.

One slug whizzed past and struck Giancana in the back of the head. He stumbled forward and Alex fired again. This time, the bullet entered his neck, and he collapsed. Giancana's body bounced off the steps and he landed on the basement floor. Alex stepped forward and planted five more slugs in the man's skull. He only stopped when there were no more bullets in the chamber.

Alex swallowed and looked around for Anthony, who was standing immediately behind.

"You were right. We didn't need a baseball bat."

"Wipe your prints off that fork and bowl, and let's get out of here."

THE MEN SAT in silence in the limo as Michael drove them back to the same fleapit where they'd stayed the night before. The next morning, they dropped him off at O'Hare and four hours later, he was in a taxi and on his way home. The pain in his chest had remained while he was in Chicago, but he had continued to take his meds and they had kept the worst of the discomfort at bay.

Alex tipped the driver well and walked to his front door. He fumbled in his pocket for his house keys and realized that he had gone straight from the hospital to Meyer's before he left Miami and didn't have them on him. He smiled to himself and coughed, covering his mouth with his fist.

When he glanced down, there was a pool of red dripping from his fingers. Alex rang the doorbell and placed his other hand on his stomach. Blood oozed through his shirt.

The door opened and there stood Sarah. Alex grinned and fell to his knees before his body hit the ground. A muffled woman's scream and then everything turned black.

42

POP. ALEX WALKED along the street and entered the garage with Ezra and Massimo. A glance at his watch told him it was February fourteen. He put his hands in his pants pockets and found the two guns nestling there. The butt of each one was cold to the touch, but he gripped them anyway.

Entering the joint, there were two guys with their heads under the hood of a black sedan and a bunch of others farther away. One of his crew revealed his police uniform, and the mechanics edged toward the back wall. Before Alex could figure out what was going on, tommy guns appeared and his men strafed the brickwork, leaving a mass of bodies in their wake.

He stepped toward the massacre and watched Sam Giancana's face on top of the pile, eyes looking upward, mouth agape, as though he were shocked to find himself in that Chicago garage on St. Valentine's Day. The more Alex stared, the more he wondered what Sam was doing there too. He blinked and…

POP. ALEX OPENED his eyes, and he was running down a street with Sarah holding tight to his hand. A mob of angry locals was chasing them. Always gaining distance, nearer and nearer. They ducked into an alleyway to catch their breath.

"Where have they come from, Alex?"

"Who knows, but they don't appear friendly."

She smiled and tugged him farther into the darkness of the narrow walkway as the men hurried along the road. He took shorter, more shallow breaths.

"I don't feel I can make it, Sarah."

"Of course you will. After all we've been through, do you believe that a Cuban revolution is going to stop us now?"

He smiled, and they hugged in the chill of the night…

POP. ALEX SAT down at his usual table in the bar, but there were strangers among the boys in his gang. For the first time, there was an Italian in their midst.

"His name is Massimo, but he only speaks Italian."

"Fat load of good that's going to do him around here."

Everyone at the bar laughed, even Massimo, who just wanted to fit in. Alex discovered he spoke Yiddish again, the language of his family. They had fled the Cossacks only a couple of years before, and here he was berating an immigrant. Shame on him.

"I have done things of which I am not proud."

"What's that, Alex?"

"Nothing, Ezra."

He knocked back a beer in a single glug and then ordered a round of drinks for everyone.

"Lechayim…"

POP. ALEX OPENED his eyes and there was white light everywhere. He shut them again to take the sting out of the brightness. Somebody squeezed his hand. He squinted and saw Sarah's outline. Behind her were a host of others, but he couldn't make out who they were.

Alex raised his eyelids a little and saw his beloved Sarah standing next to his bed, one palm in his, while she spoke to a man in a suit.

"What are his chances, doctor?"

"We've put him on a morphine drip. That way, he should be comfortable, but the news is not great. You and your family need to prepare yourselves."

Sarah turned away from the matching jacket and pants and faced Alex. When she noticed his eyes were open, she smiled and sat down.

"Don't talk, Alex. They're feeding you oxygen through a tube and it goes down the back of your throat."

At the mention of his mouth, Alex realized how his lips were dry and cracked.

"Water…"

Sarah dabbed his lips with a swab and allowed a few dribbles to enter his mouth. He swallowed and it hurt. She was right; there was no way he was going to talk now.

David appeared from the other side of his bed, leaning in.

"Hi, Pop. You don't have to worry about the family business. We are taking care of everything. I love you."

Then tears ran down the cheeks of his grown son. Alex mouthed "Thank you." and closed his eyes.

ALEX AWOKE AND swallowed. Sarah was still by his bedside. Seeing he was conscious, she smiled.

"Hey there. You've been out of it for a while."

He dragged his tongue over his ragged lips and Sarah tilted a cup of water for him to sip a little.

"The tube?"

"They took it out last night because your breathing improved."

"*Oy vey mir*. My chest hurts."

"Your stitches came out, and they had to put you back together again. I'm not surprised you ran away instead of seeing me first."

There was a glint in the corner of her eye and Alex knew he was not being told off. He searched left and right, but there was nobody else in his room.

"Where are the boys?"

"It's early, Alex. They're at home and will be over once they've had breakfast."

"Sarah, I'm not sure it was Giancana."

"What?"

"Even to his last breath, he claimed he was innocent. Perhaps it wasn't him and, besides, Ezra and Massimo admitted to me they had considered putting a hit out on me."

"Relax, Alex. At some point in everybody's life, they have wanted you dead, but that doesn't mean we all did it."

"Even you?"

"When you left me all those years ago. Of course, who wouldn't? But I did nothing about it. Most people don't."

"So you still believe it was Giancana?"

"All I know for certain is that we are all safe and you have nothing to worry about."

"*Shayner maidel*. Forgive me, Sarah, for all that I've put you through."

"You did what you believed was necessary to keep us out of harm's way."

Alex scratched his elbow and found a tube taped to his arm.

"What's this?"

"They're pumping you full of drugs. That way, they could help you feel better while you were asleep."

"Can you get word to Ezra and Massimo?"

"Whatever for, Alex?"

"I must hand Vegas over to them."

"You've already done that."

"Have I? It's hard to remember things sometimes."

She held his fingers and he squeezed. Then a door opened and David appeared.

"How's he doing?"

"They've stopped feeding him oxygen, but they kept the morphine drip going."

"Hey, you two, I am in the room."

"Sorry, Pop. You seem much better than when I left yesterday."

"*Boychik*, I feel like crap."

A stabbing pain ran across his chest, and he swallowed hard. Then he noticed his right side ached. When he opened his eyes, he couldn't focus well. Both Sarah and David were fuzzy around the edges.

"We live together, we love together..."

Alex shut his eyes to ward off the pain in his torso. He clenched his eyelids tight as the voices of his wife and son faded away from him. One breath in... All he experienced was the rasping of the air passing out of his lungs. Out...

The hurting in his chest subsided and a warm pleasure spread across his body. Alex Cohen had nothing to worry about anymore.

THANK YOU FOR READING!

Get a free novella

Building a relationship with my readers is the very best thing about writing. I send weekly newsletters with details of new releases, special offers and other bits of news relating to my novels.

And if you sign up to the mailing list I'll send you a copy of the Alex Cohen prequel, The Broska Bruiser. Just go to www.leob.ws/signup and we'll take it from there.

Enjoy this book? You can make a difference

Reviews are the most powerful tools in my arsenal when it comes to getting attention for my books. Much as I'd like to, I don't have the financial muscle of a New York publisher. I can't take out full page ads or put posters on the subway. (Not yet, anyway).

But I do have something much more powerful and effective than that, and it's something that those publishers would kill to get their hands on.

A committed and loyal bunch of readers.

Honest reviews of my books help bring them to the attention of other readers.

If you've enjoyed this book I shall be very grateful if you would spend just five minutes leaving a review (it can be as short as you like) on the book's page. You can jump right to the page by clicking www.books2read.com/mensch.

Thank you very much.

Leo

SNEAK PREVIEW

In Book 1 of the new Jake Adkins PI series, I Confess…

Jake Adkins read his newspaper, much as he did most mornings in his office. His feet rested on the corner of his desk, and he balanced the paper on his outstretched legs while he sipped a mug of java. He went back to front, starting with the sports, onto the funnies and then he tried to get through as many of the news stories as he could manage before boredom took hold and he stared out of the window of his serviced office.

The place comprised two rooms–his inner sanctum with two chairs for clients, and a couch for when he needed to contemplate the complexities of a case with his eyes shut. The other space was occupied by his secretary, a blond young thing whose main tasks were to prevent riffraff reaching the inner sanctum, and to do whatever paperwork was necessary to keep the cops and the IRS off his back.

Rat-a-tat-tat on his door and Sylvia popped her head into the room–Jake had yet to invest in any modern technology like an intercom.

"There's a woman who wants to see you, but she won't tell me what it is all about. Are you in?"

Jake threw his newspaper under his desk and pulled his tie back up to his neck. Then he whipped on his jacket which was hanging on a hat stand near a wall.

"Does she look dangerous?"

Sylvia glanced into the reception area and then returned her head into the inner sanctum.

"I wouldn't say so, although she might have a concealed weapon."

"As you are talking to me, I'd say that I am in and you should show her in."

Sylvia nodded and closed the door. Ten seconds later, it opened again and she led in a dame wearing a fancy cream skirt suit and a wide-brimmed matching hat.

"Mr. Adkins, I need your help in a delicate matter."

"Call me Jake, all my friends do."

"You misunderstand, I don't want to be your friend; I want to hire you as a private investigator."

Jake beckoned at a chair and the dame sat down. As she did so, he admired her curves in all the right places.

"Let's start from the beginning, Miss…?"

"Mrs. Avril Langchamps."

As she stressed the first word so assertively, Jake glanced at her left hand and noticed an ill-fitting wedding band.

"Are you from around here?"

"I have lived in California all my life. My parents have French ancestry, but that isn't important."

"Then what is, Mrs. Langchamps?"

"I was arrested last night on suspicion of murdering my husband and I need you to prove that I did it."

To grab your copy, go to www.leob.ws/iconfess.

OTHER BOOKS BY THE AUTHOR

Alex Cohen

The Bowery Slugger (Book 1)
East Side Hustler (Book 2)
Midtown Huckster (Book 3)
Alex Cohen Books 1-3
Casino Chiseler (Book 4)
Cuban Heel (Book 5)
Hollywood Bilker (Book 6)
Alex Cohen Books 4-6
The Mensch (Book 7)

Jake Adkins PI

The Case
I Confess (Book 1–Due 2022)
Habeas Corpus (Book 2–Due 2023)
Luther's Diamond (Book 3–Due 2023)

The Lagotti Family

The Heist (Book 1)
The Getaway (Book 2)
Powder (Book 3)
Mama's Gone (Book 4)
The Lagotti Family Complete Collection (Books 1-4)

All books are available from www.leob.ws and major eBook and paperback sales platforms.

ABOUT THE AUTHOR

Leopold Borstinski is an independent author whose past careers have included financial journalism, business management of financial software companies, consulting and product sales and marketing, as well as teaching.

There is nothing he likes better so he does as much nothing as he possibly can. He has travelled extensively in Europe and the US and has visited Asia on several occasions. Leopold holds a Philosophy degree and tries not to drop it too often.

He lives near London and is married with one wife, one child and no pets.

Find out more at LeopoldBorstinski.com.

Made in United States
North Haven, CT
03 August 2023